HOTEL VICTOIRE

HOTEL VICTOIRE

Oliver Stanley

Book Guild Publishing
Sussex, England

First published in Great Britain in 2007 by
The Book Guild Ltd
Pavilion View
19 New Road
Brighton BN1 1UF

Typesetting in Garamond by
Keyboard Services, Luton, Bedfordshire

Printed in Great Britain by
CPI Bath

A catalogue record for this book is available from
The British Library

ISBN 978 1 84624 129 1

Hôtel Victoire

You would have thought that on my first night back in the City of Light, I'd have celebrated. I might have drunk a bottle of vintage Bollinger, danced down the Champs Elysées, and then made love to a couple of wild women. One at least. Instead, I climbed into my luxurious hotel bed, and fell asleep. Then, in my dreams, my Paris friends and acquaintances began to appear ... I was delighted to see Monsieur Henri standing and smiling in the hallway of his hotel, dressed in his black morning suit with striped trousers and silver tie. He was asking with his usual quiet politeness: 'Monsieur William, you are English, so you are perhaps interested in buggery or flagellation?'

In response, I heard myself carefully explaining to my host, that, although I certainly was English, neither activity had the slightest attraction for me. I was telling him, in my best French, correctly using the conditional tense, that I would prefer instead to accept his kind offer to accompany him one Saturday evening to number 122 rue de Provence. The girls there, he claimed, were not bad. Not bad at all... And they were clean. Apparently, there was a reassuring notice in each room saying that they were inspected regularly by the Paris health authorities.

At that point I awoke and, still only semi-conscious, stumbled into my bathroom, living and breathing the Paris of half a lifetime ago. Or was it only yesterday? Some slippage had occurred in the ordinary process of memory, jumbling past and present. Once upon a time ... I'd been a penniless student, who washed his own socks in the bedroom bidet; a resident of this city, part of its structure and society. Today I was an outsider, a rich tourist, staying at The Georges V in an absurdly pompous suite with a

1

private bathroom. The taps were gold plated and the ceiling decorated with cherubim and seraphim. Which was reality, and which was recollection – not in tranquillity – but in turbulence? I splashed cold water on my face, blinked in the mirror and dragged myself fully, if temporarily, into the present. In a flash of certainty, I knew I'd made it back to the City of Light, the pilgrimage promised for months – no, years! The flight from New York and arrival late at night had left me tired and drained; sleep had been intermittent, with long intervals of discomfort for reflection on the anxieties of life and frailties of the body. Still remembering Paris as it had been, I looked out of my window, onto Avenue George V. This was the long anticipated moment. Could it now be actually happening? Or was it another preview drawn from memory? No – this time it was undoubtedly for real. I flopped back into bed and, lost amongst muddled memories, a whole episode began to form: one of the tales Henri used to tell me about Paris life during the German Occupation in the forties, an event then still fresh in his mind. In everyone's mind. We were sitting in Bar Victoire, a modest café close to his hotel, having a quiet drink. He'd obviously told this story countless times, but varied it occasionally to add dramatic interest. In this version, he claimed he'd sheltered a good friend – an old Jew called Rosenberg – in his hotel. They had been sitting with the café owner in this same bar arguing about the war.

Henri began:

'You see, Monsieur William, we were so engaged in scoring points off each other that we didn't observe the German patrol approaching. All six of them crowded into the small café, neatly stacking their rifles and helmets in the umbrella stand and shouting for coffee. They glared at us with clear hostility, if only because we had the best seats in the window. If they could find a reason for arresting us, they would. The patron disappeared to make the coffee, leaving Rosenberg and myself at the table looking silently at one another. I was paralysed with fear. Surely they would see my companion was a Jew, and would ask us for our papers. The fact that I was with him would be enough to make them arrest me. The penalties for harbouring Jews were severe. We listened to the Germans' conversation without understanding it, but from their gestures and laughter we guessed it was about girls. One of them made an open gesture with both hands, representing two full breasts, and the others whistled and nodded appreciatively. The corporal in charge seemed to have a few words of French which he was determined to ventilate. He looked at us, got up and came over. For a moment, he just stared, which was terrifying. I was sure he was going to ask for our papers.

Then he said: 'French girls are very beautiful.'

'Yes.'

'We like them.'

Rosenberg and I nodded silently.

'Is there a good brothel in your street?'

Rosenberg said: 'I don't know. I'm a married man.'

The German roared with laughter!

'So am I. So am I. We are all married men!'

He translated this witticism for the benefit of his comrades. They laughed, gulped their coffee, shouted 'Auf wiedersehen!', paid, collected their gear, and went out. At the door, the corporal hesitated. Sweat poured from me. Then he just nodded amiably and went out. The patron sat down with us again and picked up the threads of the conversation as if nothing had happened. But it had been a terrible moment.'

Still trying to remember the conclusion of Henri's story, I shifted position – easily done because I was alone in a king-sized bed – and struggled to compose body and mind in harmony, so as to recapture what had been my waking dream.

It was 5.30 a.m. and just dawn. My room was on the first floor frontage of the hotel, so I could watch the municipal refuse collection team at their important work and hear their friendly insults echoing across the Avenue.

'*Ce couillon-là est vachement moins salaud que toi!*'

'*Mais tu es le plus con!*'

3

Yes, I thought, it's I who am the most stupid.

After getting back in bed and trying to sleep for ten minutes, I opened the window and joined in.

'*Allez se faire foutre!*'

'Fuck off, yourself!' they yelled back.

I relished the familiar sounds of the language, and turned over some supplementary insults for later use. Then, dropping back on to my pillow, I tried out some of those famous literary clichés: '*It's a long time since the last time I saw Paris.*' That had been over thirty years ago! 'Gay Paree' it had been called then, but you couldn't say that now. The city had always provoked shallow, sentimental imagery, like: '*... since I saw the splendid chestnut trees in glorious blossom along banks of the Seine*' or: '*... Le Pont Neuf glittering in the summer sunshine.*' I'd always considered myself immune from all that cheap nostalgia.

Despite its well-documented charms, it wasn't the city but its people I'd come back to see. What would they be like after an interval of thirty years, those characters who had made such a great impact and whose images remained so clearly with me? Would they have retained all their friendliness, warmth and charm? I sat up in bed, abandoning hope of sleep, and tried to visualise them: Monsieur Henri standing with a welcoming smile in the hall of his hotel; Ann-Marie, Henri's sexual partner, whose charms had been obvious; Henri's terrible old mother, whose malevolence had made me physically flinch; J-P, ambitious young medical student, setting himself to make his way in the world at all costs. And, of course, the gorgeous Jacqueline, my first and longest love. I summoned up their faces in grainy black and white, like an old movie with English sub-titles.

'When I'd first gone to New York,' I recalled, 'I'd sent post-cards to all those friends in Paris, and I got one back from Henri, with a new picture of his beloved hotel – The Victoire – on the back. It looked smarter than I remembered. Henri wanted to know if I'd met again that lovely, large American lady, Madame Ida, and could I, perhaps invite her, on his behalf to

4

come again to Paris to stay as his guest? At the very least, could I find out her address so he could invite her himself and apologise for his "fragility of spirit" when they last parted?'

From my new perspective, Henri's aspirations had seemed pathetic. A year later, I'd got another card saying my replacement as tourist guide had arrived, and he was unsatisfactory. Maman had been ill and the cost of baguettes had now reached an absurd level. But by then Henri and his world had become remote, and I failed to reply. Our friendship had lapsed. In retrospect, that had been a terrible error ... but it was useless feeling guilt about it. Better instead to go back to sleep.

The next time I woke I ordered breakfast, one of the great joys of la belle France. But somehow, this morning the coffee and croissants were not quite as good as they'd formerly been. Cold and stale. So much for the Georges V! Or was it that I'd lost youthful appetite?

Then, in accordance with a carefully conceived plan of action, I picked up the telephone and dialled my friend's hotel – The Victoire. After several rings, I got a response and said: 'Can I speak with Monsieur Henri Rouget?'

'No. He's not here. What do you want?'

'My name is William Soames. I'm an American friend from a long time ago. Does he still live at that address?'

'Yes he lives here. But now he's ill in hospital and cannot be disturbed.'

'How is he ill? When will he be home?'

'Who can say? If ever. Au revoir, monsieur.'

'No, wait, listen. Give me the name of his hospital, so I can contact him.'

'It's the St-Jean de Dieu. In Montparnasse, you know.'

'Thank you.'

I hung up, recoiling from a hospital visit. Ironic that Henri, too, was ill. The recollection of white-coated doctors and nurses, bed-pans, saline-drips and body odours provoked a flicker of gastric pain. I found it impossible to envisage my friend, Henri, stretched out in bed. When I'd last seen him, he'd been young and vigorous. I suppose he'd been about thirty when we'd last met. Now he'd be nearly seventy. What could I possibly say at our first meeting? I tried out various openings: 'Bonjour, Henri. I've come back to see you after thirty years in the United States.' Or: 'Hi, Henri, great to see you at last. Let's go to Bar Victoire for a drink!' Or: 'Henri, my old friend! What are you doing about girls nowadays?'

None of those sounded practicable. While pondering the problem, I decided to go for a long walk along the banks of the Seine, summoning up all my literary heroes whose despair at their lost loves had tempted them to commit suicide in the dark and muddy waters. I had other reasons for despair, but wasn't going solve those problems by diving into the river. I turned north at Place de la Concorde, and got onto Boulevard Haussmann, at first unfamiliar. Paris was now cleaner, brighter, its streets rich in all those useless and expensive consumer goods offered for sale on 5th Avenue: Balenciaga, Hermes, Dior, Cartier. My wallet was stuffed with brand new, brightly coloured notes, but there was nothing in the shops I wanted to buy. There was no-one at home for whom I could take back gift-wrapped packages. Coming back suddenly seemed to have been a great mistake.

I turned down Chaussée d'Antin into Place de la Trinité, one of my favourite squares, and stared at the great church. Then along rue de la Victoire, pausing before the familiar façade of the Hôtel Victoire. On a plinth, niched into the façade, the stone bust of Emperor Napoleon grinned back. On impulse, I pushed open the swing door and stood in the marble-pillared hall, looking around for Henri and expecting to hear his calm, precise voice, saying:

'*Bonjour, messieurs, 'dames* and welcome to the Hôtel Victoire.'

On my first morning in Paris, I'd watched him, prototypic hotel proprietor, playing his favourite rôle of gracious, welcoming host. He would stand at his desk, elegant in morning suit, bowing stiffly at the waist, continuously smiling, his lips drawn back over his 'Clark Gable' pencil moustache, so that gold crowns emerged, and the atmosphere of his hotel polluted with the mingled fumes of garlic and tooth decay. During the post-war forties, the whole of Paris was similarly impregnated. Plus the smell of unwashed bodies and stale Gauloises tobacco: fragrances of a vanished world! Through the double doors into the marble-pillared hall had shuffled the season's first party of tourists, burdened with suitcases, weary, fearful at being 'abroad'. One lady, thin and bespectacled, a prototypic schoolteacher, clearly a sensitive creature, came much too close to Monsieur Henri, suddenly recoiled, retreated into the street and retched into the gutter. Dover to Calais by overnight *paquebot* had, it seemed, been a rough crossing. This first exposure to Europe, designed to broaden her mind had, instead, been terrifying. We all rushed to comfort her, murmuring sympathetic words, putting supportive hands round her shoulders. The effect was to produce increased spasms.

Professional crises always revealed Monsieur Henri's great reserves of strength, based on long experience. In a single balletic movement, he swept the poor creature into his *ascenseur*, slammed the gate and pressed the button, despatching her rattling upwards to her fifth floor bedroom (*'l'eau courante et bidet'*). There, alone and unloved, she was left to endure the first forty-eight hours of her *'One-Week-Guided-Whirlwind-Youth-Paris-Glamour-Tour'*, so missing the important *'Initial Information Session'* (presented by William Soames – Resident Tour Representative), and the *First-Night-Group-Welcome-Dinner-With-Red-Wine*.

After allocating the rest of my party their rooms, Monsieur Henri relaxed, grinned, winked at me and looked 'philosophical', turning his palms outwards, as if impersonating a Frenchman on the London stage. So had things gone, he implied, throughout his career.

On our arrival the night before, he had immediately confided the story of his life and his aspirations for the future.

'In 1920, I was born in the Hôtel Victoire, delivered, you will understand, Monsieur William, by the hall porter, wearing white gloves, for those had been better times for this *quartier*.'

7

'And did you spend your childhood here?'

'Yes, but my schooling was very short. As soon as I was tall enough, I started my work. I was in love with the hotel. I spent my youth in pill box hat and brass-buttoned tunic delivering messages involving secret assignations between clients.'

'Did you enjoy that?'

'Certainly. You see, I learned how to become discreet.'

'What else did you learn?'

'I learned about the ideals of courtesy and dedication, like the knights of the Middle Ages.'

'And courage?'

'Yes, courage in the face of the most intransigent and insufferable clients.'

Between the wars, the hotel had been popular amongst the jet setters of the time – if they could be called that – who had arrived at the nearby Gare St Lazare – and made a short tour of the fashionable boulevards en route. They had been rich, cultivated and Germanic. The green and gold salon still housed a row of dog-eared, Gothic script sub-erotica left over from that golden age.

'Wait until I get to the bottom of this page,' the Berlin smart set had lisped to one another. But they'd all been frozen to death at the Battle of Stalingrad, and not even their ghosts remained.

Now the hotel had become shabby, the mattresses hard, the carpets worn and catering facilities severely limited. There was no restaurant, and drinks were unobtainable. One star hotels were not so licensed. *Petit déjeuner* was simply coffee with two croissants, neither more nor less, without butter or choice. It was considered perfectly good manners to dunk them in your coffee. Tourists who insisted on tea came to regret their decision: luke warm and made with boiled milk. Each morning when Monsieur Henri personally prepared the breakfast trays you would have thought he was doing the job for the first time. Systems eluded him and he ran in and out from the impenetrable staff quarters to the salon, carrying one cup or one spoon, muttering to himself:

'...What is clear is that the circumstances of my birth have been a fearful handicap to me. Conception in chambre no. 14 – the bridal suite – birth in the salon and, ultimately, death in the kitchen...' He disappeared into it and returned with a single spoon. '...I have become no more than a piece of furniture in this hotel ... a depreciating asset in Maman's business balance sheet, waiting for the date when I am finally written down to nil. Part of its fabric and history...'

'Could we have breakfast now, please?'

'I shall remain trapped here for ever. No, wait, the theoretical possibility of escape undoubtedly still exists. I must cling to that thought ... but it would require some exterior force to disengage me, perhaps a lovely girl, with whom I can go off into a new life...'

'Could we get breakfast now?'

Reluctantly, Monsieur Henri dragged himself back from the world of his imagination into polite reality.

'One moment, please.'

He openly admitted he and his Paris hotel were in the dying throes of an unhappy love affair.

'You will understand, Monsieur William, that Paris, the City of Light, exercises a centrifugal pull on all Frenchmen. We come here in spite of ourselves. In my case that power has exhausted itself, and soon I shall go to the country, and spend my days fishing by the river...'

Tall, dark, saturnine, almost swarthy in complexion, Monsieur Henri believed that shaving was an operation not to be lightly undertaken. Once every three days was the cycle he favoured, but this may have been a practice left over from the war when razor blades had been in short supply. Memories of this traumatic era still lingered. During the Occupation of Paris, high ranking German officers had been billeted at the hotel, and he had been frequently summoned to explain which particular victory the name of his hotel celebrated. This had called for some tact on his part, but he'd apparently succeeded in convincing the Generals that the only historic victories the French nation cherished were those against their common enemy – the British. Monsieur Henri's daily uniform also dated back to a pre-war period: striped pants, black jacket and silver tie. All worn and grubby around the edges, conforming neatly with the carpeting in his hotel. Gradually, it emerged that job satisfaction had been undermined by a secret ambition.

'My true destiny is to pursue a career more valuable than that of a mere hotelier, less commercial, so as to live a finer life. Sometimes, it seems the life I seek might be found in the depths of rural France, on the banks of the river Loire, for example, an idyllic world, to which I hope to return together, perhaps with a loving wife...'

'But you were born in Paris, you told me?'

'Yes, but I am a peasant at heart. All Frenchmen are.'

'Really?'

'My natural home is in the country. Life there is more pure. I shall also cultivate my garden, using that expression literally, you comprehend.'

'Will you retire?'

'No, I have a secondary profession, which will become a new centre of activity for me.'

'What is that?'

But our conversations were continually interrupted by the demands of his first profession, so the second remained a mystery. Callers, mainly ladies, came in the afternoons to see him in his room on the first floor, leaving quietly half an hour or so later. It seemed unlikely they were all on hotel business. Was he the leader of an international spy ring? Or, from force of habit, still a member of a resistance movement? On reflection, this last hypothesis seemed unlikely, since German officers had, he'd confided, been billeted in his hotel. More likely a black marketeer or a disgraced collaborator.

Most of our conversation was fragmentary, so our friendship grew slowly. It was a one sided exchange of information, as he never asked personal questions. For him, the British were a remote race, whose mysteries he was fearful to penetrate.

Once, however, he said, 'There is one thing about your country which excites my curiosity.'

'What is that?'

'Please describe to me the taste of that English drink called beer.'

'Have you never drunk beer?'

'Never. In France, we regard it as a foreign drink.'

Henri's sole relative was his old mother, whose existence he hardly acknowledged. 'Maman' was deeply widowed, and invariably wore a dress made up of the material used during the recent war to make air-raid 'black-out' curtains. Her prominent chin was covered in hairs, and her demeanour conveyed a deep malevolence towards the world in general. This attitude subsumed her son, her employees, and her clients, particularly the British. Most particularly me. That any of them should ever have been allowed to trespass into her hotel was an intolerable imposition.

I was to discover her malice could be ferocious. She never condescended to leave her private realm, certainly not to visit the neighbouring Bar Victoire.

There, the atmosphere was cordial. Amongst the smoke and fumes of stale wine one met neighbours for gossip and *vin blanc sec*. Handshakes all round were obligatory, two or three times a day. Special privileges were accorded to tourist guides, if correctly introduced. Vicarious spending power guaranteed polite respect and *vin ordinaire* on the house. Membership of a club – an inner circle of *habitués* was automatically granted. The local barber, Monsieur Emile, graciously offered me both haircuts and contraceptives at discounted prices, whenever I should require them, adding, 'In our *quartier*, Monsieur William, there is, you will agree, a certain sense of community solidarity.'

'You are most kind.'

Overcharged to pay for our drinks, my tourists rubbed shoulders – and other things – with the *poules de luxe*, who frequented the quarter. They were identifiable by their day-shift costume: floral print dresses, laced ankle boots, and handbags. Their statutorily allocated zone of activity was *les grands boulevards*: Haussmann, Italiens and Capucines, and they stopped for refreshing drinks in late afternoon, when coming off duty. At about aperitif time, the night-shift replaced them. They were similarly attired, with the addition of moulting fur fox wraps. Price levels – even allowing for trade discount – were too high for my travel expenses sheet.

My curiosity about Monsieur Henri began to focus on his taste in girls. It was satisfied when, next day, in the Bar Victoire, he introduced me with a flourish to his current favourite, a dark, squint-eyed creature with huge breasts, and a certain brutal charm.

'Monsieur William, I would like you to meet my little friend, Mademoiselle Ann-Marie, whom I visit regularly on Saturdays. We discuss the world's problems together.'

'Monsieur Henri is an interesting conversationalist.'

'Enchanted to meet you, Mademoiselle.'

'Because I am célibataire,' he explained, 'I need a small but important physiological relief from the tensions of hotel life. The demands of my Anglo-Saxon clients sometimes become insupportable. After a correctly timed sexual emission, my normal consideration and patience returns.'

It wasn't easy to respond to this confession.

'Is that only during the tourist season?' I asked.

'Certainly. In the winter I am sometimes so relaxed, I cannot erect myself fully.'

'That must be very disagreeable.'

'I assure you it is.'

'For both of us,' Ann-Marie said seriously.

Henri expounded in some detail the coital positions he preferred, but the French I'd learned at school now became inadequate. Mostly, Ann-Marie seemed to present herself as a target to be aimed at, rather than as an intimate companion.

He added 'The atmosphere at no. 122 is quite relaxed. Do you not agree, Mademoiselle?'

'Certainly.'

'Like an English club, I have been told. One meets a number of fairly distinguished people there. Members of the government, you know. I have found Monsieur Auriol to be very unassuming... It was gratifying to recall that I had voted for him as President. There are opportunities to exchange ideas with people, to expound political views. It is a companionable place.'

'Really?'

'I would like, if I may, to invite you to accompany me sometime. It would be a valuable experience for you. A social occasion. And it would enlarge your knowledge of the French language. Clearly, you would be present there as my guest.'

'That is most hospitable of you.'

'The girls are all inspected regularly.'

'Monthly.'

'I am certain, Monsieur Henri, that I would enjoy the experience.'

The familiar marble pillars were still there in the hall. But there were new carpets and an unpleasant smell. Fresh waves of nostalgia. A black man in a dirty shirt stood behind the reception desk.

'You want good room?' he asked in English.

'No, I'm looking for someone. Monsieur Henri Rouget.'

'He not here now.'

'He was the owner when I came here years ago.'

'He not owner now. I ze owner.'

I looked round the hall while the owner picked his nose with great care.

'You want a girlie? Take room for one night, and I get you French girl.'

'No thank you.'

'Nice girlie. Very clean.'

'No.'

'You want young boy? Give you big suck?'

'No.'

13

'OK. Then you fuck off?'

Outside, Napoleon was still on his plinth, but the Emperor was now preoccupied with other matters and refused to meet my eye. Attempting to recapture the past had undoubtedly been a colossal mistake. Why hadn't I been content to let Paris stand as it had long been – a set of vague and agreeable memories?

My second day in Paris – I recalled – had coincided with a key date in the glorious history of France: *Quatorze Juillet*. In order to help me in my demanding day's work, Henri had given me his précis of events.

'You may not be aware, Monsieur William, that the course of history is often affected by climate. On 14 July 1789, weather in Paris was hot and oppressive. In consequence, wine flowed freely, affecting the mood of a hostile crowd gathered at Bastille to demand release of political prisoners. The Bastille, as you know, was part of the old city walls, a prison surrounded by a moat. History books relate that Monsieur de Launay, the prison governor, invited leaders of the mob to join him for a gastronomic lunch. This, he believed, would surely pacify them. Alas, the soup was cold. From inside, his guests pulled down a drawbridge so that crowds could surge into the courtyard. Guards opened fire, and the French Revolution, destined to continue for twenty-six bloody years, got under way...'

'So it was the lunch, not the weather?'

After he'd dealt with an angry telephone call, he continued.

'Yes, both. The storming of the Bastille was a muddled and confusing affair. Events occurred out of sequence. First, De Launay threatened to blow up the garrison. Then he put out a white flag, surrendered and had his head cut off, which was subsequently paraded around on a pike. Later, it was deposited at a police station against a written receipt, so securing for him a place in history books. The fallen Bastille was demolished, and thus a great symbol of absolutism in France had been heroically conquered!'

After dinner, I managed to escape from Henri and my tourists, and set off alone. One hundred and sixty odd years later, it was disappointing that not a single remnant of the prison remained in the square. The rampant centre column had not, I discovered, been erected to record events of 1789 but, ironically, to celebrate the July Revolution of 1830, which put Louis-Philippe onto the French throne. Around it now danced a circle of young Parisians, laughing, shouting and singing their hearts out: great fun for them, but difficult for a lonely, self-conscious Englishman to join in. Then the circle opened hospitably, and lovely girls in light summer dresses smiled and beckoned. To refuse them would be churlish. After we'd all whirled around hand in hand, the music faded, the dance ended abruptly, and everyone turned and kissed the nearest girl – innocently, because it was *quatorze juillet*, when you celebrate being French, and no other reason is needed. Kissing seemed an agreeable way of establishing a relationship with strangers. The tall, dark girl I had clumsily kissed tasted of wine and roses, which were delicious.

She laughed and said, 'My poor little boy! You looked so isolated standing watching us. You mustn't remain alone on *quatorze juillet*. We shall adopt you.'

'That's very kind. You for your part all looked so happy, singing and dancing, and celebrating the glorious history of France.'

'Are you a foreigner?'

'Yes, I'm British.'

'You're teasing me. I don't believe you. You speak good French.'

'No, really I am!' I said in English.

This engaged her attention and that of other girls who clustered around to examine this strange phenomenon.

'Say something else in English for us!'

For a moment, I couldn't think of a word in the beastly language. Then, in a flash of inspiration, I recited:

'On with the dance! let joy be unconfined;
No sleep till morn, when Youth and Pleasure meet
To chase the glowing hours with flying feet...'

15

'That poetry,' said my new friend, 'is by Lord Byron. What a romantic fellow he was! Surprising for an Englishman.'

This was impressive.

She went on. 'He was a very great writer. Do you admire him very much?'

It seemed difficult to conduct a penetrating discussion about the Byronic muse in the middle of the square and, anyway, music and dancing were starting again. Seizing my friend by the elbow, I shouted to her, 'Let's go and get a drink.'

For a moment, it seemed doubtful whether she'd come.

'All right,' she said, grabbing her two friends by the hand, so that the four of us formed a line.

'We'll dance over to that café on the corner.'

Once wine had been ordered, we introduced ourselves. My special friend, Jacqueline, was a beauty with long flowing hair and a wonderful smile. But her chums, Louise and Bernadette, were hardly less attractive. Louise had dark eyes, and a terrific figure. Bernadette was a classic specimen. I could fall hopelessly in love with all three. No, I already had! Setting out alone to find adventure and friendship, I'd been received by the Three Graces: Euphrosyne, Aglaia and Thalia, goddesses of beauty and grace, who disbursed joy and gentleness. Or rather Hera, Aphrodite and Athene. I was cast in the rôle of Paris, son of Priam, appointed by gods to judge amongst them. This childish fantasy was soon extinguished. They were students at the Sorbonne: smart, sophisticated, able to discuss life and books, with enviable fluency. Soon, refreshed by wine and conversation, they were ready to move on.

'Let's go,' they shouted, 'to rue de Lappe.'

This was an alleyway of *bals musettes*, behind Place Bastille. It was a relic of fin de siècle Paris, a cross between dance hall and cabaret where, traditionally, gangsters took their molls, men danced in caps, famous apaché dances were invented, and you could have a girl for ten francs and still get change. But on *quatorze juillet* all working class Paris was packed happily into the narrow street. We pushed our way into a hall with a rough wooden floor. Trestle tables round the sides were crowded with drinkers, all absolutely silent and immobile. On a stage, lit by a blue, flickering spot, stood a small, dark, plain girl singing:

> *'Ce soir, il y a bal dans ma rue*
> *Et dans le petit bistrot, la joie coule à flot...'*

There was a burst of applause and she disappeared unsteadily into the wings.

'She is formidable,' they told me.

'She is called "le Piaf" – the sparrow – you know. She is a girl from the streets, who loves life and men, and wine. Particularly wine. But she sings like an angel, does she not?'

I conceded that she did.

Couples crowded onto the dance floor, holding their partners with one hand, the other behind their backs. The accordionist played:

> *'La fille de joie est belle,*
> *Au coin de la rue la bas.*
> *Elle a un clientèle*
> *Qui lui remplit son bas...'*

> 'On the corner of that street,
> There's a gorgeous tart.
> She's got clients,
> Who're making her rich...'

Soon, after more wine, we were on the move again, whizzing through unknown streets on the open rear platform of a 28 bus. No tickets needed on *quatorze juillet*. On each corner we passed crowds singing and dancing, some attempting a palais glide, others cheek to cheek in a tango. Brass bands competed with accordionists. *'A la Bastille!'* they shouted as our bus passed. Or: *'Vive la France! Vive la république!'*

17

We were headed for a sector with a different style: *Quartier Latin*. This was where my new friends lived, and loved. Music and dancing in Place St Germain des Prés was louder and wilder. Here cafés had all put up shutters, but bottles of wine circulated freely. Girls and boys were dressed in bizarre clothes, so you couldn't tell one from the other. A line of masked figures suddenly ran through the dancers shouting incoherently and waving dangerously lighted torches. They came very close, and Jacqueline threw herself into my arms for safety. I very much hoped they'd come back.

'Is it always like this – the *quatorze*? Do you come here each year?'

'Last year we came here to this square and danced through the night. My boyfriend was a great dancer,' she said seriously. 'Not like you, William, with your big English feet!'

'Where is he this year?'

'I have lost him.'

This was really good news! Now clowning and horseplay had faded, and couples were turning closely together in time with slow music. Jacqueline put her head on my shoulder and I brushed her dark shining hair with my lips. It was one of those magic eternities which can only be captured by poets. I had been offered all kingdoms of the world in a moment of time. Then she turned her face to me and we softly kissed, not for the first time but for the first time with any meaning. We looked at each other, and I thought that it had never been like this before and never would be again.

'*Tu es vraiment gentil...* You're nice: like Lord Byron, but not, I think, such a bold seducer as he was.'

'Don't be so confident.'

She didn't smile. This joke was too English for her. I thought of another few lines written by his lordship and spoke them aloud:

'She walks in beauty, like the night
Of cloudless climes and starry skies;

And all that's best of dark and bright
Meet in her aspect and her eyes:'

This was very well received. She laughed and said, 'Your feet may be clumsy, William, but your tongue is not.'

We sat back to back on a street bench, between dances, not saying much, but content with each other's company.

Then, disconcertingly, she said, '*Il faut que je m'en aille…* Now I must go off and meet my friends. They will be waiting for me.'

'I'll come with you.'

'*Non, non, je suis en retard.* No, it's late. We must part now. Tomorrow, I have my early lecture.'

'Wait, Jacky. At least tell me where you live. You can't just go off like that. Can't we meet again sometime? We've only just started talking.'

Suddenly, she came up close, kissed me on the lips, gave me a quick hug and, before I could grab her, rushed off into the crowd. Hesitantly at first, then with growing desperation, I struggled to follow. The street was crowded with tall girls with long, flowing, dark hair – but none of them was the right one! Which way had she been going? Back towards the Sorbonne? I half ran, half walked, east along Boulevard St Germain as far as Odéon. Here the crowd had thinned, but there was no sign of Jacqueline or her friends. She might have turned towards the Seine, along rue St André des Arts. I tried that. No use. Should I go back to Place St Germain? There seemed no point now. In Place St Michel dancing continued, although it was two o'clock in the morning. A sense of depression began to overwhelm me. What an absurd end to my night! It had all been as muddled and confusing as on the original *quatorze juillet*. What crazy behaviour! Perhaps her charm and friendliness had been just for a ball, and at midnight she'd had to return like Cinderella to her hearth. Had she, perhaps, gone off to look for her 'boyfriend', who danced so incredibly well? Had I said something to offend?

19

I began to reconstruct the whole evening's conversation for clues. All I knew was her first name and that she was a student of literature in her third year at the Sorbonne. That would make her about twenty. Where did she live? It was clear I'd lost her for the rest of *quatorze juillet* – or rather *quinze juillet* – but had I lost her for ever, a girl with kisses tasting of roses and wine, with a marvellous open smile, who read Byron and who'd welcomed me into the dance?

All the music had by now ceased, and the last lights of the city were being turned off. In Boulevard St Germain before me stood the statue of Georges Danton, a leader of the revolution. Famous words were engraved on his pedestal, a rallying call to France in danger: '*L'audace, l'audace, et encore l'audace…*'

It was difficult to summon up much boldness by this stage. Anyway, Danton had had his head cut off, hadn't he? So all his courage hadn't done him much good. Once more lonely and homesick, I began the long walk back across the river to my narrow, lumpy bed in Hôtel Victoire.

Now what came flooding back was the detail of Henri's personal life, which he began to disclose after our friendship had been cemented by tourist crises confronted together. I'd found this very flattering. He had, he said, 'financial problems'. Maman acted as treasurer and controller and dealt with all hotel correspondence. Distrusting banks, accountants, taxmen and, above all, Henri himself, she kept cash takings in a huge iron safe which stood challengingly in her hotel bureau. Weekly, at 6.00 p.m. on Saturdays she was to be seen ceremonially unlocking it with giant keys kept on a chain around her waist, in order to give Henri and the *valet de chambre* – who worked a twelve hour day – a few francs wages. We all watched, whilst Henri – always patient – stood over her smiling and breathing for quite a long time before she unbuttoned a black leather bag. It was a procedure conducted in silence. As notes reluctantly changed hands, we were tempted to applaud. And while the ritual was in progress the hotel desk remained unmanned. Tourists were jostling at it for information, reservations, or to get a good view of the spectacle.

Once Henri started talking he couldn't be interrupted. Sometimes he became, alas, a terrible bore, but in the first few weeks of our relationship he kept me enthralled. He was not alone, he claimed, in yearning to return to the pastoral life. 'The girls frequenting the boulevards are all from the provinces. They stay in Paris only for a few dangerous years. Their objective is to put together a fund of capital to be invested in a small town business. A café, or a husband, or both. They too practise serious economies.'

'Really?'

'Unfortunately, their pimps take a large percentage.'

'Why is that?'

'It is traditional.'

'Really?'

'Yes, and it is a share expressed in both cash and kind. Unfortunately, their economic contribution is small in proportion to the large percentage that they take.'

He wagged a finger in the air.

'A much greater equilibrium is needed between effort and reward if France is to prosper as a nation in the post-war world.'

'I'm sure you are right.'

By the evening of the first day I needed to escape from my surroundings. Retreating into the dusty salon of the Victoire, I sat reading and relishing the fictional city of Paris described so enthusiastically by that amiable idiot, Lambert Strether in *The Ambassadors*.

'The air,' he claimed, 'had a taste of something mixed with art, something that presented nature as a white-capped master chef.'

That was before he learned that, in Paris, his friend's son, Chad, whom he'd gone to rescue, had got involved with a naughty lady, Madame de Vionnet. At first, he thought they met in the afternoons to drink tea. Then, he found out that they were having it away on the chaise-longue in the salon. At least twice

21

a week! Or more often! And Chad was enjoying it, and hadn't the slightest intention of giving her up! Worried and disillusioned, poor old Strether heads back to Boston. Paris is a dangerous place, he'd discovered.

Now my tourists were gathering around like hungry flies, and it was time to close my Henry James and take them out to the 'First-Night-Welcome-Dinner'. This ritual engagement would demonstrate that on a WHIRLWIND TOUR no expense is spared; that the dried eggs and whale meat diet of post war Britain had been left behind; that they would be spoiled for choice, because in Paris there's a family owned restaurant on every corner, with menus – hand-written in purple ink – offering a three course meal for 150 francs, including a carafe of fruity red wine and a handshake from the patron.

They would be taught that restaurants and cafés perform different functions. Restaurants involve the serious business of food. You never eat in cafés. You sit on the terrace, with a cooling drink, waiting for your friend to arrive, watching the world go by. You are known there; you call the waiter by his first name. It is your second home. In a cynical ballad that's where the boy waits for his girl every day for forty years. She never comes. In the last verse, he sees her in the café opposite, married to the owner. He'd been sitting in the wrong café! Well, *merde!* That's life!

It would have been convenient to have led my batallion to Le Trou Normand, an inviting and popular establishment, directly opposite the Victoire. But *la patronne*, Madame Poublade was apparently Henri's greatest enemy.

'I assure you, Monsieur William, that she is corrupt, and disgusting, serving unspeakably tough beefsteak, and watered wine. Respectively comparable to soles of old shoes on a plate and gnat's piss.'

'Really?'

'Really! My earnest counsel is to go elsewhere. I would recommend Chez Robert. I will effect the introduction, so that a helpful arrangement can be made.'

'What might that be?'

'It will ensure that one gets all meals gratuit plus a demi-carafe of red wine ... in the capacity of *agent de tourisme*, of course.'

'Of course.'

Henri's feud with the Poublades was a source of entertainment for both protagonists and the whole *quartier*. It was born of some ancient encounter involving unpaid return commissions, complex percentage deductions, and a public shouting match, during which both sides were urged on by supporters. Madame Poublade was a keen businesswoman. She would have offered me the hand of her lovely daughter – or any other valuable part of her anatomy – in exchange for a guaranteed regular flow of business but, alas, fate had thrust us into the camp of enemy forces. We exchanged quiet smiles and murmured *bonjours* when Henri wasn't watching.

Chez Robert, the whole family was heavily engaged in the business. On arrival it was obligatory to shake hands all round, and exchange pleasantries. This agreeable ritual took some time, and initial warmth and charm was liable to turn to anger and contempt. Tourists who had not eaten all day became impatient with this first delay – and worse was to follow. The problem was that each dish was prepared and individually cooked only when ordered, so that by the time it was served, steaming and delicious some forty-five minutes after the orders, a state of mutiny had been reached.

'Inefficient, that's what it is, Mr Soames.'

'Never seen anything like it.'

'Can you smell the drains?

'Those people came after us, and they're already getting their puddings.'

'You should complain, Mr Soames.'

'Tell them we've paid in advance.'

'It doesn't take this length of time in my fish and chip shop at home.'

'I expect they've run out of something.'

There was no appeasement until food appeared, and then the problem began to resolve itself. Although eating had a pacifying effect, the unfamiliarity of the menu created new problems. On this first night, colossal linguistic misunderstandings had to be resolved, eccentric tastes explained, a cultural chasm bridged. Raw salads of tomatoes and cucumber, sluiced in oil and vinegar would, it was claimed, cause 'wind'. Beefsteaks and mounds of *pommes frites* were more acceptable, despite their being 'bloody' within.

'Half-cooked, they are!'

'Too lazy to cook them properly!'

Three important art-form categories – *seignant*, *à point* and *bien cuit* – had to be explained and learned. And there was the startling practice of washing it all down with *rouge de la maison* served in earthenware jugs. This was rejected at first as harsh and rough, but became progressively more palatable as the hours rolled by and they began to recount adventures of their day, boring for everyone save the storyteller.

'We were caught in the French rain,' Mrs Polianski told me. 'And we sheltered in an arcade. A reely nice French guy told me we were trapped like the animals in Noah's Ark.'

Her daughter added, 'He wanted to carry Mom across the road.'

'Did she like that?'

'You bet.'

'What happened?'

'They wanted to buy her drinks. I just tagged along.'

'Did they speak English?'

'Sure. They told her they were French knights rescuing a foreign damsel in distress. They expected to be rewarded with at least a kiss. Or an afternoon in a hotel. All that romantic stuff. My mom reely went for them in a big way. One of them said he wanted to keep her in his country house as a pet.'

Mrs Polianski was a large, extrovert lady from New York or

Chicago, clearly a trouble maker, destined to be a source of complaint and catastrophe. She was followed everywhere by her daughter Trudy, a thin, sycophantic shadow. Mr Polianski, we were given to understand, had long since fallen by the wayside. He had also been called Henry.

Towards the end of the evening, Monsieur Robert appeared from the kitchen, sweaty and beaming, conscious of having bestowed his culinary favours. The clink of glasses served as a fanfare of trumpets signalling his arrival. He lit a Gauloise, and exchanged handshakes with regular customers. Congratulations were offered and accepted. Some of his neighbours took all their meals in his restaurant and regarded it as their dining room. Short and fat, like many chefs, Monsieur Robert was a genial and popular host.

Mrs Polianski was quick to grasp the situation.

'Hey!' she shouted. 'It's the chef.'

Heads turned.

'What a great meal! Those French Fries were reely sumpun. And that sour cream. Wow! As good as my deli on 53rd Street.'

A cheer leader is what every tour party needs. Monsieur Robert grinned and nodded to us. He didn't need any English to recognise that he'd been voted hero of the hour. He bowed as best he could to Mrs P, who rose in her seat with difficulty, stepped forward and seized his hand. Monsieur Robert, raising the stakes, pressed it gallantly to his lips and we all applauded. The next move should have been *la bise* – the pecks on the cheek – but a problem presented itself: Monsieur Robert's bald dome reached up only to Mrs P's large bosom, so he would have needed to have stood on a chair. The awkward silence was relieved by Maurice, the accordionist, who opened nightly with:

'Chantons la vigne,
La voilà la joli vigne,
Vigni, vignons, vignons le vin...'

25

Mrs P grabbed Robert and, clutching him tight, wheeled him round in her version of the polka. Ignoring Madame Robert, who had been watching doubtfully from the wings, I swept up Sylvie, the seventeen-year-old waitress, whose prominent black, sateen bum presented itself as an attractive objet d'art, and we whirled into the dance together. In a burst of post-prandial entente cordiale, tourists and regular customers seized one another wherever they conveniently could, and lurched around, in a tiny space, knocking over chairs and terrifying the cat, which ran screeching into the kitchen. Maurice, delighted with his success, played faster.

'De vigne en terre,
La voilà la joli terre,
Terri, terrons, le vin...'

Even a thin, shy girl in my party, whose name no one remembered, had found a partner. Or he found her. A villainous old Italian with an eye patch grabbed her round the waist, swinging her backwards, so that she collided violently with his brother. Some kind of disengagement followed, but later the thin, shy girl disappeared. That was worrying. Had she been exported to the Street of a Thousand Poppies in le Maghreb? Should I notify the police? No, later in the evening, the two Italians returned her safely to the Victoire, they shame-faced and apologetic, she somewhat the worse for wear, but radiant from her experience – whatever it had been...

The music stopped long enough for us to gulp wine, change partners and start off again in a valse:

'Under the bridges of Paris with you
That's where I long to be...'

Sylvie snuggled closer and my right hand gently caressed her bottom, a delicious texture, firm but soft, the contour unspoiled by any underwear. When Maurice went into Latin-American mode, Mrs P climbed onto a table, twitching her shoulders and swinging her skirt in time with the music. The table appeared to be in grave danger but, before it collapsed, Monsieur Henri appeared from nowhere and helped her down.

He shook me by the hand – the one not pressed on Sylvie's hospitable bottom – and shouted, 'I am practising my knowledge of the English Language.'

'Good.'

'When I was a pupil, we were taught a difficult English locution to help us master the strange sounds. Can you tell me what it means?'

By this time, Sylvie had been swept from my clutches.

'What?'

'... an English locution?'

What is it?'

'*My tailor is very rich.*'

It took a few seconds to recognise he was speaking English, and to grasp the meaning of the words.

After my translation, he said, 'Aha! I know that in your country tailors are an exceptional class. The Englishman takes care of his clothes, the way a Frenchman regards his gastronomic experiences. In my family village...' Henri seized me by the arm, so preventing a return to the dance, '... they told the story of an English officer, who had hidden there from the Boches during the war.' (He meant 1914–1918). 'He was always properly dressed. His manners were absolutely impeccable. Unfortunately, he was preoccupied with the English vice. At the end of the day, he was arrested and imprisoned. That would be typical, would it not?'

'No.'

'But there are many of your compatriots who practise the vice, are there not?'

'Excuse me, I must...'

'Come, my friend, admit that you yourself...'

'Let's go and dance,' I said. 'Why don't you invite Mrs Polianski?'

'That is an interesting idea. I think I will.'

So I never discovered what he meant by 'the English vice'. Was it buggery? Or flagellation? Sometimes, I thought it would be easier to tell him I regularly enjoyed both!

My next day brought more new revelations about Henri's life and loves. The dusty salon provided a perfect location for eavesdropping, justified by language students as part of their learning process. Conversation in Maman's office – mostly about failure of moral standards – wasn't difficult to overhear, because it was exchanged at full bellow. In one afternoon a dozen reputations could be destroyed. It was educative, more rewarding than my studies of irregular French verbs.

At about three, Maman received with unaccustomed civility a formally dressed gentleman, sleek and bearded, who'd arrived clutching a brief-case stuffed with documents.

'My client,' he was saying in measured tones, 'is well placed to be of assistance in the refurbishment of the Victoire. Her resources are in liquid form, or are readily convertible, and she has accepted the need to make a secure long term investment.'

'How much has she got?'

His reply was bland.

'The amount of cash available is for discussion at a later stage, but you may rest assured it would be adequate for the purpose.'

It appeared the Rougets were contemplating the introduction of a new partner into their hotel business. Moth-eaten chairs and peeling wallpaper would be smartened up. That would please my tourist agency. The next series of questions didn't fit with this hypothesis.

'How old did you say she was?'

'My client is thirty-six years of age, but she looks younger, having lived a healthy, agreeable and trouble free life – trouble free until the death of her late husband, that is. She has a dignified and serious personality.'

'When did he die?'

'Three months ago. By now, my client has recovered from the

shock and grief of his parting, and is ready to begin a new life. I am confident she would make an excellent partner for Monsieur Rouget – in both the commercial and personal senses, of course.'

'If it's only three months, the affairs of his estate can't have been resolved yet.'

'Not finally, of course, but as there were no children of the marriage there can be no dispute about my client's inheritance.'

'What about death duties?'

'You may rest assured that is a matter which is being dealt with.'

There was a long silence, while Maman reflected on the proposition that had been put to her, whatever it was.

Then she said abruptly, 'Come back next Tuesday, and I'll give you my answer.'

'Certainly. I am confident you will perceive that this represents an excellent refinancing opportunity, with obvious benefits for all parties involved.'

'Including yourself.'

'In that connection, may I leave you this small document, explaining my business terms?'

'Next Tuesday at five.'

'You'll naturally discuss my proposals with Monsieur Henri?'

'No, that won't be necessary.'

'But madame...'

'My son will do what I tell him, which is all that need be said.'

'If I may advise you, Madame, from my long experience in these situations...'

'No, you most certainly may not. Until Tuesday, Maître Roustain.'

'Au revoir, Madame.'

So Henri's matrimonial future was about to be settled. In his absence and without his being consulted. As if he were a youth of nineteen rather than a confirmed bachelor of thirty-five. But perhaps it was the custom in France? As a deal, it was well-balanced. Henri

29

would get the girl, Maman would get the dowry to invest in the hotel, and the widow would get a new husband. But I felt anxiety on my friend's behalf. Would he be willing to accept that bargain according to Maman's dictate? On the basis of my knowledge of him, it seemed unlikely that marriage to a widow of thirty-six would accord him the elusive satisfaction with life that he sought. Should I try to warn him that a plot was being hatched?

When, next afternoon, Monsieur Henri was sitting with me in the salon, and opportunity for conversation practice arose, I casually observed, 'According to my reading of Balzac, marriage can be a very happy state. Other writers make out the opposite case. What is your considered opinion?'

This was a question calculated to provoke a full response and it succeeded.

'You may well ask, William. I have reflected many times upon the issue from various standpoints. *En principe*, the state of matrimony has much to commend it. Daily companionship, the combination of meals prepared in one's own kitchen, and regular fucking to be enjoyed comfortably in one's own bed, free of time based costs, would seem an attractive proposition. And there is the possibility of procreation, of reproducing one's kind. That would be an interesting experience. And essential for the continuation of the human species.'

'Have you ever contemplated such a step?'

'An interesting question. Approaching the same problem from a more pragmatic – what you might call typically English – standpoint, I have never yet encountered a lady who has attracted me sufficiently. Sufficiently, that is, to make me willing to spend the rest of my life with her. I am not clear why that should have been so. Perhaps it has been because my opportunities for meeting lovely girls are necessarily limited by my profession.'

'But lots of girls come and stay here at the Victoire.'

'Yes, but they are clients. It would be unprofessional for me to consider them as future partners.'

'I see.'

'In any event, they are all foreigners.'

'But you have other friends?'

'Very few. Maman is not, as you know, a very sociable person, and we do not entertain.'

Our conversation was interrupted by a new guest waiting to check-in, so further revelations had to be postponed. For some days the forthcoming marriage was not mentioned. In any event, I was preoccupied with the Saturday night excursion: the breath-taking climax of the 'One-Week-Whirlwind-Youth-Glamour-Tour' – a holy pilgrimage to La Butte Montmartre, a shrine of the past, whose charm was not yet extinguished. It was still a hill-top country village, soon to transform itself into a film set of cut-out cardboard cafés and restaurants. On the previous Saturday, the departure point for this excursion-at-no-extra-charge had been fixed at another historic site: rue d'Amsterdam, behind Gare St Lazare, a street where Daudet lived, loved, drank and occasionally found time to write. There my congregation had gathered to be preached a first sermon: not to get lost, robbed, kidnapped, raped, and certainly not all four on the same excursion. This was calculated to provoke a shiver of nervous excitement amongst the girls, contemplating – for a happy moment – the proverbial fate worse than death. To prolong this sensation of pleasurable terror, it was helpful to pause outside Grand Guignol. This ante-dated Beckett's Theatre of the Absurd, and might have been styled 'Theatre of the Obscene'. Its blood curdling atrocities were off-limits for tourists. Already on an earlier tour, Monsieur Henri had had to cope with the results. A honeymoon couple succeeded in scaring themselves witless. They had rushed out of the tiny theatre during a celebrated scene in which a pious and half-naked nun is violated and strangled by two monks on an altar, a supplementary ecclesiastical element being considered to add extra dimension to eroticism. Faced with a case of babbling hysteria, Monsieur Henri simply cracked his patient across the face with open palm. This immediately silenced her. She sat down and said politely, 'Could I have a cup of tea, please, with milk and two lumps of sugar?'

'It is best sometimes, to avoid sophisticated medicines,' Monsieur Henri commented with satisfaction.

On the following Tuesday, I positioned myself carefully, awaiting Maître Roustain's arrival. Unfortunately, after he'd entered Maman's office, he turned and meticulously closed the door behind him, so that only a murmur of voices could be heard. Sometimes those voices were raised in anger or protest so that occasional words could be distinguished. Maman's bass voice repeating 'Not enough! Not nearly enough!' filtered through, but any general sense of the conversation was lost. After an hour and half, Maître Roustain emerged, looking severe, but happy. It appeared a deal had finally been struck.

This fact was confirmed by Henri himself a few days later.

We were sitting together at his usual table in Bar Victoire, when he began: 'Mon cher William, following our interesting conversation about marriage, I am going to take you into my confidence, and tell you my new problem. You will be surprised, believe me.'

So Maman had told him his fate. And he was resigned to it.

'Good news, I hope?'

'No, no, not at all. Maman has found an investor, who has agreed to produce the capital sum necessary to refurbish the Victoire. It would acquire a new lease of life. You will have perceived the need for some interior decoration, but what you will not know is that the western wall was examined last year and found to be bulging outward. It needs to be strengthened and underpinned. This is quite a major renovation. So quite a large amount of investment is correspondingly needed. Amounting to several millions of francs!'

'So you will get a new partner in your hotel business?'

'That is the problem, for this new investor is a lady who would become my wife.'

'Congratulations. And is she very beautiful?'

'Thank you very much. As to her charms, I cannot say, as I have not yet had the pleasure of meeting her.'

32

'I see.'

'But a meeting has been arranged for some time next week.'

'You'll be looking forward to that.'

'There are advantages, evidently. As well as being a working partner in the hotel, my wife-to-be would be a companion for my mother, who is lonely from time to time.'

'Evidently.'

'And for me.'

'Where would you live?'

'What do you mean?'

'Where would you make your matrimonial home?'

'I will continue to live in Room no. 2, and I have been thinking that Room no. 7 might serve for Madame. It has always been difficult to let – because of its odd shape, you know.'

'Won't you want to share a room?'

Henri looked startled at the prospect.

'No, no, not at all. I couldn't do that. If I agree, it would be on a business basis. It is not my intention that marriage should disturb my settled way of life. I couldn't have another person living in my room, which I use for consultancies, and where I keep all my medical books and case histories.'

'I just thought room sharing was usual in marriage.'

'Perhaps you are right, in principle, but this marriage would be exceptional.'

'Anyway, Room 7 would not be far to go at night.'

Henri looked even more startled.

'I don't think you understand, my dear William, the nature of this marriage. It is to be a marriage of convenience only. The lady in question is far too old to be interested in night-time fucking. She is a widow and will have had her fill of that activity during her previous marriage.'

'So you would continue to see Ann-Marie?'

'Certainly.'

'On Saturday nights as usual?'

'Certainly. In fact, Maman has agreed, in response to my

request, and as part of the whole transaction, to substantially increase my monthly emoluments, so it may be I shall be able to visit my friends at no. 47 more often than once a week. And there is another club which I'd like to join. I anticipate putting a lot of financial problems behind me from now on. After the wedding it would be my pleasure to invite you to join me at no. 122. In my new circumstances, I will no longer accept any refusal, my dear William.'

'Thank you.'

'But I still have to decide...'

At that moment, as if to illustrate alternative delights, Ann-Marie and her best friend Georgette came into the bar and made straight for us. They were in their working finery but somewhat dejected, having spent the afternoon trudging Boulevard Haussmann without any success. After we'd exchanged greetings, and bought the girls a round of drinks, Henri continued his previous conversation, as if they'd not been present.

'You must understand that the net effect of this change, my dear William, would simply be to benefit the hotel. As Maman has pointed out, it would be disloyal of me to refuse to marry when our enterprise is in grave jeopardy. The dowry is badly needed for a very important purpose. I cannot afford to risk the collapse of the hotel structure. And, of course, it is not as if I were love with any one else...'

'No.'

Of course, it would have been helpful to have produced a son who could take over management of the hotel.'

'After your life-time?'

'Or earlier, so allowing me to retire to my village on the banks of the Loire.'

During this exchange, the girls had been listening open mouthed. What, I wondered, did Ann-Marie make of all this?

On my rearranged Montmartre tour we avoided Grand Guignol and set the first staging post on Boulevard Pigalle, named after the absurd fountain in the centre of the square, sculpted by one

J-B Pigalle. Here you could have all the fun of the fair: bumper cars, candy floss, and multi-lingual fortune tellers, whose promises of dark strangers were calculated to bring blushes to the cheek:

'E come to you in ze night. You wait for 'im. E say: "Embrace you: zat is what I do." You give 'im big kees. E put is arms around you. E old you close to 'im. E give your body big feel … ver' exciting.'

'What is his name, please?'

'E no speak name.'

'What will he be like?'

'E very big. Big arms. Big legs. Big cock – all for you.'

'Oh Angela, did you hear what she said?'

The next leg of this voyage of discovery was up an acute-angled *ascenseur* to the white onion dome of Sacré Coeur, from where you could absorb the floodlit history of the great city: Arc de Triomphe, Nôtre Dame, Invalides. Then into Place du Tertre where ghosts of Raoul Dufy, and Henri Matisse regularly appeared, set up easels and in a few brush strokes, captured the charm of the square. Now another pause for drinks and a headcount, because one young couple was reported missing. Presumably, they had wanted to be alone together, under the moonlight, dazed by accordion music. Understandable – but would they ever find their way home? I began to worry about them.

To include an authentic Frenchman in these tour parties always added excitement. On this occasion, Jean-Pierre, a young friend of Henri's – tall, bearded, and handsome – came to ventilate his English and his personality.

He confided: 'My important medical studies do not go well, you see, because my professor is not sympathetic. He is envious of my skills. I am very artistic with the knife. For the surgery, you understand. He does not appreciate that. So I am needing a small holiday.'

During our walk he talked relentlessly of the United States, a promised land, where he would live, practise medicine, make his fortune.

When we had all got a glass of wine, he said, 'Now I tell you a story about my big romantic experience. Here in this square, I meet a lovely girl. I pick her up. I say to her: "Why are you so sad and so beautiful?" She reply: "Because I am alone, I have no one to speak with." So I say: "You speak with me." She answer: "All right." We go to a night-club where we dance and drink. We laugh like children together.'

Serious, and totally self-absorbed, J-P had the manners of a great Manhattan physician, lacking only the commitment to acquire medical skills. His father who supported him was caretaker at the Victoire, and worked day and night. J-P accepted financial dependence as if it were his right.

'... She has come to Paris with her parents from Boston. They are not at all *sympathique*. She told me I should not like them. They are not kind to her. She has escaped from the hotel by climbing down the fire escape...'

Now the whole party fell silent and started to listen to him.

'... She has fallen in love with Paris, and wants to live here for ever...'

Like all good story tellers, J-P knew when to break off.

'What happened?'

'I have been with my friends. They have all passed the first year practical physiology. I have failed. I am feeling bad, you know? They all go off, so that I can be alone with her. Because I want to fuck her, you know, but I never do...'

'You respected her too much?'

'No, no, not at all. It was we had nowhere to go. See that *boîte* over there.'

He pointed to Le Lapin Agil, a small cottage painted countless times, a perfect setting for romantic experience.

'We went just there. It was good. She don't speak French, and I don't speak American too well, but we fell in love OK. She say to me, "Geese, geese"!'

'What did she mean?' one of my tourists asked.

'I don't know too well. I think maybe birds were flying over.'

36

'No, she wanted you to kiss her.'

'Oh yes, I do that, certainly.'

'What happened then?'

'We kiss. I tell her my life story. We are sad together. We dance. I feel her breasts. They are very firm. For me she is everything I want from life.'

'What made you think so?'

'She is so perfect. American, you understand rich – but innocent and beautiful. She is in love with life. For her it is good. She has no duties, no studies, no examinations. She is free like a bird, flying over Paris.'

'Perhaps it only seemed like that because she was on vacation.'

'At dawn we went to Les Halles – the market, you know – and played together amongst the flowers. She herself was like a flower – so pure. Then we were hungry, so I took her to Au Petit Cochon for onion soup and *vin d'alsace*. It was a good vintage year, I remember. We sat close together and she put her hand in my trousers. That was very nice. But we had no money to pay the bill, so they threw us out. We laughed at them. Then they forgave us, because we were young and so much in love. We walked hand in hand back to her hotel, the Ritz in Place Vendôme. She told me that she loved me and that she wanted us to be together for always.'

'Those old clichés!'

'It was all true, I tell you. It was a perfect romance.'

'Which, normally, only occurs in books.'

'Only in Paris...'

'Yes, only in Paris.'

'What happened then?'

'I left her at the hotel. We wanted to fuck together and perfect our love, but she said she could not.'

'She wanted to keep herself pure?'

'No, not all. I tell you it was because there was nowhere we could go. She asked me to come for her the next day. At noon. We would meet. We would plan to run away together. I told her we would go first to my cousins in the country. They would receive us. We would work on their little farm. Then we would go to Boston. Her family would forgive her because they would be happy to see her again. I would complete my studies. She would get money to keep us from her father. She would help me become a great doctor. Then, when I became famous and rich, we would come back to Paris.'

There was another prolonged silence as his audience contemplated how this fairy tale would end.

'What happened then?'

'I went home, but I could not sleep. I lay in bed all morning thinking about her and our life together, which would be so beautiful. Time passes slowly when you are in love but, mon dieu, separated from the one you adore... At noon I went to the Ritz Hôtel. First I waited, then I went to the desk and asked for her. He looked at his book. They had checked out at eleven. One hour before. I never saw her again.'

J-P bowed his head, so low that it almost touched the table.

'This square has reminded you of her?'

'Yes! Such was my absolute despair, I at once decided to join the Foreign Legion. But I couldn't do that under my family name because it would have embarrassed my father...'

J-P burst into dramatic sobs, so that people on the next table turned to look. Being British, the rest of us were discomforted by this display of emotion and pretended not to notice.

After a few minutes he recovered and said, 'Let's go to Le Lapin Agil now. There we can dance and sing, and I shall forget.' I paid the bill, and we all got up.

He whispered to me: 'William, you must help me find her. When you go back to America, will you search for her?'

'I'm not American. I'm English. I've never been to America.'

'Is that so? Well, shit, there's plenty more American girls in Paris, aren't there?'

That was one celebrated image of the city: The Youthful Romance of a Summer Night. Most Parisians were happy to spend a few agreeable moments recollecting their hour of stolen kisses and unforgettable passion before departing, often with their screaming children, to their second homes in the country or on the coast. In August, only tourists remain in Paris, wandering in groups through the tourist shrines, pausing to take pictures, and getting lost.

Clearly, intellectually enriching experiences were certainly not to be found on the Grands Boulevards. I would need to penetrate unfashionable *quartiers*, out on the periphery, territory of the dispossessed, in urban squalor. Here – I'd been told – dwelt fine artists, bold anarchists, the true aristocrats of Paris, who wore their poverty proudly, like a badge of courage.

To find them, I walked north towards Clignancourt, behind the onion dome of Sacré Coeur, a *quartier* off limits to tourists, where the tap dancing Americans in Paris never ventured. The filthy streets around Boulevard de la Chapelle recalled for me the novels of Zola. Here Gervaise waited all night for Lantier, surveying from her hotel window the steaming slaughterhouse of Boulevard Rocheourt and the Laboisière hospital emitting dreadful odours. She imagines her lover stabbed to death, but he gets home safely, after a night with two other girls. When she complains, he beats her up.

Somewhere in this slum was a shrine of Art and Culture to which I had brought an offering: a packet of English Rich Tea Biscuits. 'If you bow low,' my introducer had said, 'keep your back to the wall.' The shrine was located at the top of a dilapidated apartment block. I climbed the staircase, which smelled strongly of pee. In the proverbial garret the worshippers sat in a semi-circle around their Leader. This was the famous Wise Old Prophet, a typical Englishman abroad, long exiled in Paris: The Count de Santi.

His face was deeply lined and tragically haunted. Grey matted hair fell to his shoulders, which were swathed in a black woollen shawl. His voice was high and plaintive, expressing justified grievance against Fate, which had dealt him a terrible hand.

During the afternoon he smoked through a packet of Gauloises, lighting each from the stub of the last and sticking it into a long ebony holder.

My offering of Rich Teas vanished into a cupboard. One of the young male acolytes surrounding the Prophet handed him a cracked cup, whilst another recited a poem:

'Poète, prend ton luth; le vin de la jeunesse
Fermente cette nuit dans les veines de Dieu.
Mon sein est inquiet: la volupté l'oppresse...'

The Old Prophet closed his eyes to contemplate the wine of youth fermenting in the veins of Our Lord. This caused him considerable discomfort, and he started so violently that a tube of ash from his holder fell into his tea. It must have improved the flavour because it was made French style with boiled milk, luke-warm and quite disgusting.

The incantation died away for a ceremony of initiation into the brotherhood

'Why have you come?' the Prophet asked me.

'I have come for tea.'

'Where have you come from?'

'Straight from my hotel...'

'No, no, where have you come from?'

It was tempting to make some facetious reply, like: 'I come from haunts of coot and hern.'

'From England.'

'What is the true source of your being?'

Clearly, the time had come to seize the initiative. It was necessary to concede that the source had been darkness, a state of ignorance, but one was aspiring towards a finer way of life. One understood that he and his friends met to contemplate mysteries, discover eternal truths, and perhaps one could attend and listen from time to time and even, with his permission, participate later?

This seemed to approximate to a correct response. Rites of

passage were passed. I was told: 'You will come next week, and bring a fruit cake with raisins.'

The discussion then became general. The question was put as to whether Time Present was indeed Time Future, and whether the Force did indeed drive the Green Fuse. At the end, The High Priest, or whatever he was, delivered a short sermon. It was, he said, important to be graceful in life. Gracefulness would produce a state of Grace. This aphorism provoked murmurs of appreciation. Shortly after that, worship ended.

The most forthcoming acolyte said, 'My name is Frederico. I come from Bradford.'

'Pleased to meet you.'

'The Count has taken a special liking to you.'

I had no answer to that.

'I'm also in the travel business. Could I come to your hotel to discuss things?'

'Certainly.'

'Would you introduce me to the owner? I might put some business his way. On a commission basis of course. I'm looking for seven and a half percent.'

'Of course...'

Because of the demands of my profession as tourist guide, it was some time before I could go again to Clignancourt. For my tourists, Paris, in this era, was an ideal city in most respects: romantic, decaying, grimy, over-crowded, rich in museums and culture, with great scope for overspending. One English pound bought over a thousand French francs. But it suffered from a fatal flaw: total inadequacy of sanitary facilities. *Les lavabos, les doubles vécés, les cabinets de toilettes* – whatever you called them – were all hopeless, lacking every amenity. Doors failed to lock, flushes to flush, lights to light, lids to open. Complaints and protests never secured comfort and satisfaction.

Public lavatories were to be avoided save *in extremis*. Parisians penetrated their nearest café – one on every corner – and headed unerringly for a door, often unmarked. They were in-and-out, without even a '*Merci, Monsieur*'. For foreigners, this was a daunting test: one had to ask, 'Which door?' By misunderstanding, or perverseness, you might be served a large cognac. Sometimes, a request for '*la salle de bains*' produced a stream of invective.

Another hazard was *toilette turque*, translated as 'crouching crapper'. This required correct positioning to avoid toppling backwards into an unspeakable pit, a manoeuvre to be performed in total darkness, holding door closed with one hand, under-garments in the other. Sacred shrines were always guarded by ancient priestesses, demanding exorbitant offerings before worship and, afterwards, fees calculated in centimes per sheets of paper. Costly over a holiday week. Fresh confrontational situations emerged with every new tourist party, now processing at the Victoire with terrifying regularity: assembly ... roll-call ... baggage check. All reversed one week later: reassembly ... roll-call ... baggage check ... lost items found at last moment ... final headcount on platform 5 ... thrust them tired and complaining into over-crowded train ... back for a relaxing drink with Monsieur Henri ... next party's arrival. Roll-call ... assembly ... and so on.

By comparison, Henri's functions at the Hôtel Victoire began to seem ornamental. Each morning he stood bravely behind his desk, like a captain on his bridge, facing into the wind, ready to navigate through rough seas ahead. These storms were often violent, but blew themselves out quickly. They included furious complaints as to coldness of bath water, unmade beds, bedroom windows which refused to open (or close), or doors which refused to close (or open). Basin plugs were reported missing so often as to suggest some mysterious force at work.

On these occasions it was customary for the tourist guide to stand at one's right hand and help one keep the bridge. This meant interpreting, because Henri had no talent for foreign tongues. None of his clients had any language other than English, and some had baffling regional vocabulary and accents. Greeted by Northerners with: 'How are yer, Jock?' he needed to be repeatedly convinced that 'Jock' was not a term of abuse. Henri was very patient and eager to help with detailed directions for finding the tourist attractions of Paris, its monuments and shops. In this he faced two major problems: a towering language barrier, and the fact that he did not know the city, because he rarely went further than Bar Victoire or no. 122. Hence his precise directions through streets had to be treated with caution, particularly when given and received by hand gestures. Counting was practicable only up to ten, and pricing a nightmare of misunderstandings. It was better to let him go it alone, as three way conversations left everyone even more bewildered.

'You said it would cost £300?'

'*Non, non, Monsieur, trois cent francs pour aller, et encore trois cent francs le retour...*'

'Does that mean three hundred each way?'

'*Un peu près.*'

'Does that mean "yes" or "no"?'

In an effort to be helpful, Monsieur Henri sometimes switched from francs to sterling half way through, using his own rates of exchange, thus convincing tourists they had been, or would be, cheated. On such occasions, they were prompt to shout 'Foul!' and to summon their tourist guide as referee.

'This nice gentleman says I've paid too much. Would you please come back to the shop with me and tell them I bought this lovely souvenir this morning and I've been overcharged, and I want my money back?'

'For starting a row like that in Paris you can be put in prison the next day.'

'We're leaving early tomorrow.'

'Well, you can be put in prison on the same day!'

It was after Henri explained to his mother that I was teaching him English that Maman began to view me with suspicion. The fact that I was a foreigner was, in her eyes, inexcusable. Insular, chauvinist, and dominated by ruthless self-interest, she conveyed to me that, in her view, my homeland was outside the boundaries of civilisation. She obviously hated hearing Henri using the few English phrases which he had retained from his schooldays. Sometimes, as an experiment, he would casually ventilate one of these to any client prepared to listen.

'I am telling you, Madame, my tailor is very rich.'

Mrs Polianski found this puzzling.

'Well, honey, if your tailor's rich he didn't get that way making the suit you're wearing. Is that the latest Parisian cut?'

'Oh yes.'

'With that double-breasted veskit?'

'Oh yes.'

'Well, honey, they stopped wearing those in Chicago in 1932.'

'Oh yes?'

'How long have you had that? Since the Wall Street crash?'

'Oh no.'

'Listen, can I get tea with lemon right here?'

'Oh no.'

Not being directly involved in running his hotel, he had time to formulate elaborate theories about the nature of the universe, which he expounded to me. He was confident his reasoning always advanced by logical steps, so that conclusions were thoroughly justified.

'You, in England,' he often told me, 'have your traditions. We in France, have our logic.'

Gradually, the mystery of his 'secondary activity' was resolved. When he first explained it, the word he used – homeopathy – was unfamiliar and an awkward misunderstanding occurred. All became clear when he produced an illustrated textbook on homeopathic medicine. This showed specimen patients in full frontal postures – tense before, and happily relaxed after, imbibing *verveines* or tisanes. Or in course of applying magic poultices to sensitive areas. They all bore a considerable likeness to my tourists.

'Homeopathy,' Henri explained, 'is treating like with like. It is bringing to an illness a substance which, in a healthy person, would produce similar symptoms to those displayed by the person who is ill.'

'I see.'

'We do not believe symptoms are caused by illness.'

'Really?'

'They are bodily reactions to an illness, attempting to drive it out...'

'How do you know that?'

'So we stimulate the symptoms – increase, not suppress, them. Moreover, we treat the whole person, who thus rejects the symptoms creating the illness. He becomes purified. Life renews itself...'

Once launched into his subject, Monsieur Henri's personality changed. Although tourists queued at his desk to complain about cold bath water, nothing could break his flow. All his gentle courtesy vanished, replaced by a dogmatic enthusiasm. He told me: 'It is always necessary to be "*engagé*". I am truly committed to my work as a homeopathist. If I were to practise full-time, and not only in the afternoons, that would give me a new fulfilment.'

So his afternoon callers were patients, not black-marketeers or international spies!

'If you gave up your hotel?'

'Yes. You see, William, I am not big enough also to be committed to my work as a hotelier. One must recognise one's limitations.'

'Certainly.'

'The gratitude of my patients would be rewarding in itself. But their consultation fees are also welcome, particularly since prices at no. 122 have augmented ferociously this year.'

'By a large percentage?'

'Too much. And the services supplied have not correspondingly improved.'

'That is hardly fair.'

Henri nodded agreement. 'It is deplorable!'

Another topic on which Henri had strong views was the digestive system.

'You will be interested to know, William,' he explained, 'that I am opposed to the indiscriminate use of suppositories, so fashionable in Paris at the present time. I am persuaded, following my researches, that they introduce too many foreign substances into the blood stream.'

'I don't think they're used much in England.'

'Good.'

Henri's striped pants and black jacket were an equally appropriate costume for his profession as medical practitioner. In the afternoon he seemed to wear them with more authority. As a doctor, he gained in 'presence'. Even his power of communication improved. He was certainly right about prescription of suppositories. A tourist couple who had burned their skins by spending too long at a swimming pool on the Seine had been supplied with them by a local pharmacist, without particular directions as to use. The results were unfortunate. Finding it difficult to apply the medicament as a cooling ointment, they'd decided to swallow one each before dinner.

'The wrong end,' Henri explained to them, first pointing his index figure downwards and shaking his head. Then he pointed it up and nodded violently to clarify his meaning.

He would have liked to practise more on hotel guests, and sometimes politely inquired whether their digestive systems were in good order. If not, could he, perhaps, assist? '*Comment vont vos selles?*' was his enquiry. Fortunately, none understood.

Pressed for details, he told me: 'Your daily turds are revelatory as to the quality of your digestion in three separate and important characteristics. First, there is the question of their colour, which should be a medium brown. Second, there is texture, which should be firm. Finally, there is shape, which should be fully formed.'

'Should one make a daily examination?'

'Absolutely!'

It seemed preferable to avoid discussing these topics with tourists. Conversation about stomach problems always provoked discussion about quality of hotel tap water. Sometimes this flowed with a brownish tinge and tasted metallic. Henri's advice was that it was '*potable*'. He personally had been drinking it all his life and had undoubtedly survived.

'However, in France, wine is the normal drink, and I counsel you to prefer it to water, even the purest.'

It was an era when British tourists preferred a pint of best bitter, and other familiar elements of their lives in Bolton or Birmingham. On their last day they would sit together in the salon concluding that products in Paris shops were all available at home. Quality was better there and prices lower. Real coffee, crusty baguettes and delicious patisseries could be bought in Paris for a few pence but, alas, you couldn't get a nice pot of tea and a bun anywhere. At the end of their holiday they often expressed relief that their terrifying ordeal was nearly over, that they would be returning to a familiar world. If exposure to the abroad did enlarge minds, it seemed to me a slow and painful process.

It was true that Paris wasn't London. Even in the mid-twentieth century, it remained a conglomeration of separate villages, each with its own style. In the eighth *arrondissement* there was the golden triangle: Champs Elysées; Avenue Montaigne; and Avenue Georges V. Here, everything is chic, à la mode, call it what you will. There is the Latin Quarter, renowned for philosophers, second-hand bookshops, and revolting students, who slam up barricades when they've nothing more interesting to do. They are genetically dissident and don't wash much. There are *les beaux quartiers*, the 16th and 17th *arrondissements*, where dwell aristos left over from the guillotine. But the most recognisable village revolved around Place Contrescarpe, between the Panthéon and Jardin des Plantes. It had a dusty open centre, ideal for an hour of *boules* in the afternoon, and dancing to accordion music on Saturday nights. There were friendly *bistrots* in Contrescarpe, and a complementary green *urinoir*. This was where Jake Barnes,

Hemingway's flawed post-war hero, had lived. There – not surprisingly, in his condition – he had trouble with girls, English, French and American. ('It was a rotten way to be wounded...')

Years later, nubile American lovelies still clustered in Place Contrescarpe, spilling over into rue Déscartes. They were blonde, be-jeaned, and spent their days reading *The Sun Also Rises, A Narrow Street,* and the terrible poetry of Edna St Vincent Millay. Mom had fixed it for them to soak up a slug of Yurropean culture: the gospel according to St Henry James, The Old Master, whom they found 'kinda deep'. They were all sophomores and juniors at Radcliffe and Wellesley, pursuing vacation courses, called 'World Literature' or 'The Film And Society Today'. This was a new wave of American expatriates, fascinated by the romantic idea of Paris, hating its reality, which they found dirty and hostile. To me these creatures seemed a new species: outward going, frank talking, athletic looking, sexually exciting, identifiable by their loose-legged, confident walk. But what '... really were they like?' as the Old Master would have put it. To his own penetrating question, he replied: 'Everyone in Paris shows for what they really are.' Was this true? Would Paris serve as litmus paper, capable of revealing the nature of being? What effect would it 'really' have on these alien creatures? Maturing? Corrupting? Or what? The first impression was of lost little girls, far from home, needing to be constantly reassured they were having a great time ... needing directions as to how to travel on the metro ... and through Life! Paree was OK – no better than that – but the French were inhospitable and hated Americans because they had won the war. So far, the only French guy they'd met had tried to rape them in broad daylight in Luxembourg gardens. When they'd fought back, he had expressed himself as deeply insulted, explaining that he'd simply responded to an obvious invitation.

'A linguistic misunderstanding, perhaps?'

'Not this guy. He understood the word "No!" OK.'

'I expect he was just being friendly, according to his conventions.'

'Friendly? You must be crazy. He had me in a half nelson

with one hand, whilst he was opening my blouse, and into my bluejeans with the others.'

'How many hands did he have?'

'At least eight. Like an octopus.'

Surely not all transatlantic relationships were destined to be as sour as that? In order to build one, Julie – my new friend – and I were ready to spend a whole day together in a relaxing ambience. Where to go? Having taken counsel both from J-P and Henri, the conclusion was: 'To the Woods!' We two Anglo-Saxons set off by train, heading for a peaceful village, St Germain en Laye. There, forest, flowers, birds and bees – not to mention an elegant château, would bring us happily together.

And so it proved. An isolated hollow in the woods, a baguette, a box of Camembert, and a whole bottle of rouge guaranteed post-prandial drowsiness, exchange of life's aspirations, innocent kisses, progressing to not-so-innocent kisses, followed by the opening of a blouse, to reveal small but attractively shaped, coral-pink tipped breasts, hands into each other's jeans, and all the other progressive steps that Julie had described as so totally, absolutely, unacceptable in the Luxembourg Gardens.

We joined hands on the train ride back to the city. Companionship was what we were reciprocally offering, for being an expatriate Anglo-Saxon in Paris can be a lonely life. Among a day of other agreeable reliefs, it had been a relief to talk without having to use a past participle functioning as a relative clause Instead, to recognise a common language, with books written in it. O'Hara and Faulkner and poor old Jake Barnes – the guy who had trouble with girls ... the sun rose, but he couldn't. There was still the evening stretching ahead in which to cement our perfect relationship. To balance out Paris sunshine it was proposed we visit Harry's Bar, watering hole of a smart American set.

'Some of those guys,' she said, 'come from my home State.'

'Why not wait until you're back?'

'Listen, these are guys writing about Europe with real insight. Others are assholes. It's a city bar with bench seats.'

'All the tourists of the world will be there.'
'Hell, no. The bar prices keep them out.'
'They keep me out.'
'Listen, I've got dollars.'

This was neither time nor place to fight a battle. And the hot, dark womb of the metro was the wrong arena. Here, couples clung to each other kissing passionately, oblivious of their surroundings. No one gave a second glance, for this was territory where you could lay bare your feelings and escape from prudery. Julie seemed to think she was back in the forest. At the metro station Opera, notices implied passage into a less secure world: *Au delà de ces limites, les billets ne sont plus valables.*

We exited into crowds and bright lights, at an exciting hour when pickpockets prosper. Holding each other, we pushed our way into a shouting, multilingual mass of drinkers at 5 rue Danou, widely advertised as 'zinc roo dah noo', that being the instruction which Anglophones should give a taxi driver. Here, the Real Thing to drink was Coca Cola, a beverage fashionable in the sorority houses at the University of Virginia, where admission rules were important, complex and demanding. Around us, snatches of other conversations intruded:

'... listen, you guys, flinging yourself into the long grass is never as exciting as it sounds in books...'

By comparison with the questions of etiquette as between sophomores and juniors in Richmond Va., even this was gripping stuff. Shouting across two other monologues, Julie told me, 'The first Wednesday of the semester is always election night, when you have to have a minimum of seven proposers and four seconders, at least half juniors, and they write their names on your card. Then they send the card to the Room Captains, who have a Captains' Meeting on the same night. Only that night's meeting is for the proposals of the previous week...'

'But you said it's the first Wednesday of the semester?'

'OK, OK, they get the proposals left from the previous semester in the first week, and the proposals from this semester in the last week.'

'The last week of the previous semester?'

'Hell, no, of the next semester, no – wait – of that semester...'

Daytime love and friendship was beginning to seem an experience enjoyed long in the past. A rictus grin was developing.

'Shall we go get some fresh air and a sandwich?'

'William, you just haven't been listening. The next stage is the voting round. All the sorority members have votes in proportion to their membership time...'

At such times, strong men seize their women by the hair, caveman style, drag them into a field, and silence them with the force of wild passion. Before I could do that, the door opened, and in came Jean-Pierre, two blonde sisters, (those whom J-P had repeatedly praised as talented in bed), and a large smiling person, undoubtedly American.

'William, my old comrade, what can you be doing in this den of evil repute?'

'May I introduce my friend Julie from Virginia, USA?'

'Delighted! And here is Ann-Sophie and Lorette, and my new colleague, who is called Wesley, and who also comes from America.'

'Hi folks.'

Wesley was black. He was also large – so large, that all other aspects of him became insignificant. In the dim light of Harry's Bar he seemed abnormal in both height and breadth, grotesque, a giant among pygmies. To address him you had to look up. Wesley was prototypically negro, with shaven head and gleaming white teeth. In a pageant of peoples he could have symbolised the whole African continent, Southern states of the US and West Indian islands. He had a magnificent physique and spoke slowly in a resonant bass voice. Drinkers made space for him.

'We have been showing Wesley some of the delights of Paris at night. He has only just arrived in Europe.'

Jean-Pierre, delighted to have a larger audience, addressed us in his fluent but eccentric English, of which Anne-Sophie and

Lorette understood nothing. 'We are doctors together, and we shall in perfect combination cure all known maladies. Do you have a head of pain? You must consult Wesley. He will fix it by cutting off your leg. Then you will have a leg pain, but your head pain will be completely cured.'

Wesley laughed at this joke for quite some time, and his laughter resounded around the bar like a peal of thunder, drowning all other voices.

'Ho, ho, ho, ho, ho...'

Julie, less pleased than might have been expected at meeting a fellow citizen abroad, moved to put distance between Wesley and herself. J-P, hysterical at his own wit, translated into French for the girls.

Julie said uncomfortably, 'William, I have to go now.'

This was puzzling. A chance meeting with an international party in a smart bar should have entertained her and redounded to my credit. So truly Parisian and sophisticated. Anyway, it was early, with ample time for a romantic dinner and, after that...

J-P asked, 'What have you two young lovers been doing together?'

'Relaxing in the forest of St Germain en Laye. We had a *déjeuner sur l'herbe*.'

'Was that good?'

'Yes.'

'Did Julie take all her clothes off?'

'Alas, no...'

'Then what was good about it?'

'It was good to be out of Paris, in the countryside.'

'No, no, William, it's never good to be away from Paris.'

'But cities are harsh in the summer.'

'Where do you come from, Wesley?'

'Nashville, Tennessee, man. There it gets so hot in the summer you can fry hot dogs on the sidewalk. The bluebottles are as big as sparrows, and the mosquitoes like Flying Fortresses.'

Julie tugged my arm.

'I've gotta go.'

In this declaration, there was a note of finality. We had been standing pressed up at the bar, now emptying, talk and laughter fading away. The Americans had moved on, leaving only a few French. Harry was not pleased by this sudden exodus. He began to survey us from behind his bar with deep animosity. We were clearly offensive in some way, but how? Suddenly, letting go my arm, Julie disappeared through the door, without any *au revoir*.

After her conclusive departure J-P said, 'William, you have failed to satisfy that lovely American girl. You have not been kind to her, probably because you have not been making love to her with sufficient ferocity. Many times have I told you: first you throw girls to the ground, then you rip off their clothes, then you jump on top of them. It is this sophisticated technique which you Anglo-Saxons so sadly lack. I will give you a course of lessons at the medical school. With practical demonstrations. Anne-Sophie and Lorette will play the parts of the heroines. They will be good at that.'

Spluttering with laughter at his own wit, J-P translated this fantasy into French for the 'heroines'. Wesley caught my eye.

'I guess nigras ain't too popular here.'

Behind the bar, Harry heard this and took it as his cue.

'Why don't youse guys drink up and get outta here. I ain't got nuthin against niggers but you ain't doin' my business any good.'

'Go fuck yourself.'

Even the girls could understand we were no longer welcome. Wesley grinned hugely at our discomfort.

'Don't you worry about it man.'

We gulped down our drinks and withdrew with dignity into the street. There was no sign of Julie. J-P wanted to kick a hole in the plate glass window, but Wesley persuaded him that that would be unwise. We shook hands and went our ways, each thinking his thoughts. Mine were that Strether was absolutely right: the lights of Paris do brightly illuminate, showing people up for what they 'really are'. And when people are thus shown up, they can reveal themselves as very disappointing.

Another of my profound discoveries was that Man does indeed create his own destiny. My second visit to the Prophet of Clignancourt was via a different route: rue de la Goutte d'Or, a name derived from a mediaeval vineyard, and birthplace of Zola's Nana. Now it was a North African ghetto, populated by halal butchers, from whose grisly slabs sheep's heads sneered. It was a relief to find the Count and his young friends in unrestrained mood. The salon was crowded, and pervaded by a pungent odour. Incense? The Wise Old Prophet appeared more demoniac than before. All colour had drained from his face, and one pink eye watered constantly.

'We must escape from the conventions of present day society,' he explained, patting me on the cheek. 'Here in Paris the revolutionary tradition frees us from the inhibitions imposed by our English backgrounds. That is why I have come here. That is why you, William, have come.'

'Not really.'

'We can be ourselves, find ourselves, know ourselves. We can build relationships which are true and free. Come with me into my bedroom, for I have something interesting to show you. Something for you to hold gently in your hand.'

'I'm just going to have a word with Frederico.'

'William, you charming young thing, you need to escape from your old way of life. You need true, loving friendship, the meeting of minds in a pure world inhabited only by those who have escaped.'

'He's over there, I think...'

'Have you read the works of Gerard de Nerval?'

'I don't think so.'

'Come closer. I want to whisper a secret in your ear. Have you read the works of my great friend André Gide? The sweet

54

man wanted to dedicate a book to me, but that would have been too great an honour. He wrote about masculine friendship, where there are no barriers. In our little fraternity we tell each other all private thoughts. Come, I will tell you mine; you must tell me yours.'

'I am still learning how to communicate.'

This was no longer the right reply. There was no murmur of applause from the attentive acolytes. Today they were more numerous and more epicene. The tea had been put away, and they were drinking Pernod and tap water – a dangerous mixture.

'You are young and handsome, and you are searching for friendship. I can give it to you. Take my hand...'

'Unfortunately, I have to go now as I have my party arriving soon at Gare St Lazare.'

'Take my hand...'

The acolytes crowded closer and it began to seem that 'back to the wall' was not just a crude joke. The Comte seized my hand in a flabby grip and tried to pull me closer. I stamped violently on his foot; he howled and released me.

'You revolting creature. You have no capacity for true friendship.'

'I have to go now. Thank you for tea.'

This was the moment to bolt for the door, stepping over a couple of acolytes, who had fallen to the floor, clutching one another in what the poet calls 'a wild embrace'. It was time to return to conventional, bourgeois values.

A few days later, Frederico ('Call me Fred') presented himself at the Victoire to be introduced to Monsieur Henri. Fred wiggled his bottom, and for a moment succeeded in looking coy. Then he got back to business. Soon, parcels of foreign tourists were being bought and sold at discounted prices, less commission. Fred seemed much more pragmatic than I'd expected.

'You English,' Henri told us both, when the dealing ended, 'have your long established traditions. But we in France prefer to rely on logic.'

Fred was too busy with his calculations to reply. After he had gone, Henri remarked, 'Personally, I have never found men as a species physically attractive. It is possible to be in love with ideas, buildings, artistic works and, of course, girls. Men never. But I am not entirely surprised, William, that you are now moving in homosexual circles, because I have read that most Englishmen have a suppressed tendency in that direction. It is the effect of your schooling, is it not?'

I vehemently denied the accusation, reflecting upon the other helpful Existentialist maxim of the time: 'We all construct for ourselves the kind of world we wish to live in.'

At peak of the tourist season, my overnight tour parties arrived at Gare St Lazare, each day at dawn. This was an exciting hour for new arrivals to be guided, dazed from their journey, through empty streets to the Victoire. At five in the morning, Paris drains automatically reversed themselves and street gutters flowed like crystal fountains. There was no traffic: all was peaceful, even in corner cafés where workers speechlessly gulped their morning coffees and cognacs. Upon our arrival at the hotel, Monsieur Henri was patiently waiting at his reception desk.

After rehearsing his welcome procedures and whisking them off in his lift, he whispered, 'How interesting, Monsieur William, that each of your tourist parties should be composed of such typical English specimens!'

This time, he was absolutely right. There was a pair of ripe young chicks having one last free flight, before facing their dreadful destinies. Paris, they repeatedly told each other, would be an experience to look back on. One was a beauty, the other of vinegar aspect, but having more enthusiasm for sexual adventure. Another always recognisable species comprised gangling, immature young colts, never before released from Mum and Dad, hesitant to go out by themselves, homesick for workplaces which had structured their lives. The bolder ones asked about prices of clean girls, because Paris was notorious for sexual licence. Most immediately identifiable were nice old grannies, who wanted to buy French knickers at Galéries Lafayette, and would the tourist guide go with them and make sure they got the right size? But the daily problems thus presented paled into insignificance by comparison with those set by the individual tour party of Mrs Polianski and her daughter. Their European tour boasted a processional quality, a triumphant progress from Chicago, Ill. to the Mediterranean, Paris being merely a first staging post. From the moment of her arrival, Mrs P, large and genial, followed everywhere by her daughter, had dominated hotel life.

When politely questioned about her partner, she replied, 'The hubby stayed in Chicago.'

Whether in the matrimonial home was not clear. What *was* clear was that the high standards of that home were not reproduced at the Victoire.

'M'sewer Soames, I want you to know that room 17 is kinda dirty...'

'Sir, my bath water was reely cold last night.'

'I have to make a serious complaint about your facilities: the wash basin plug does not function.'

'May I order fresh orange juice for breakfast tomorrow?'

'Can I make a collect call to Boston, USA?'

When she claimed the WC smelled, Henri's legendary patience began to falter. The possibility was denied – monosyllabically.

'Undoubtedly it smells,' I said, 'with the authentic odours of the seventeenth century Paris sewers which can be visited in the afternoons on Thursdays, between two and four p.m. Entrance is fifty francs. Nearest metro: Gobelins.'

'Bullshit!'

'Alas, the state of the sewers is beyond the control of the hotel management, or indeed of the tourist agency, but...'

'Just you come sit in it,' she insisted.

All three of us crowded in. There was certainly no room to move. The odour of garlic mingled with other fumes. To switch on the light you had to bolt the door. There was no window. It had to be conceded the atmosphere was dense and poisonous.

'How can I crap comfortably in this hell-hole?'

I translated for Henri, who asked: 'Is Madame perhaps constipated?'

'Huh?'

I translated.

'We in France are accustomed to logical solutions. The logical solution to Madame's problem is to use a particular remedy, which is very efficacious, provided the herbs have been freshly gathered. I could make up a potion. It is not disagreeable to the taste...'

There was a pause. I translated. She burst out laughing, and the quarrel was resolved.

'Is he some kind of quack doctor?'

'He is a homeopathist, and very skilful.'

'Is that so? Would you ask him about one of my personal problems?'

'Certainly, but can we get out of here?'

For a few seconds, it seemed that the door bolt had jammed and the three of us would together die a death by asphyxiation. Henri coughed delicately. Then Mrs P put her broad shoulder to the door and we burst out on to the landing, to the surprise of tourists who were forming an orderly British queue outside.

Mrs P said, 'Let's go get a drink. You guys had better come round to my place for a pick-me-up.'

'She is high-spirited, one admits,' Henri said, after we finally escaped, declining a second round of bourbon in tooth glasses.

He was in a surprisingly good humour, considering she had delivered a barrage of insults concerning his hotel and *la belle France*, particularly its water-closets.

'And generously proportioned,' he added, picking up the book he'd been reading, but staring thoughtfully into the distance.

Later that day, I realised that this had been a fateful encounter. Whilst we three had been struggling to escape from that putrid WC, Cupid had flown in – or swum in as there was no window – and had loosed his fatal arrow at Henri.

'In Paris, you understand, William, the God of Love can strike on unexpected and inappropriate occasions,' he told me.

He clearly had Mrs Polianski in mind, and it began to seem she was often in his thoughts. This conversation had begun when Henri, the Revd John Mann, another member of the current tour party and I were all sitting reading in the salon. Henri put down his book to warn me of the dangerous behaviour of Cupid. Then he set off on another of his favourite themes.

'Paris, William, has traditionally been a city of Light, drawing young adventurous moths in from outer darkness. If you were fortunate enough to have been tempted during your green and formative years you'll surely want to return in your troisième age, so that you can walk sadly through the familiar, elegant streets, recapturing the events of the past. It's not so much the city itself which you'll be searching for, but memories of your own youth: the celebrated temps perdus when you were ready to tear the heart out of life, burning for experience of a world; full of new ideas, which you wanted to absorb; full of new people you wanted to meet; great books to read; pictures to be seen; music to be heard. You'll want to relish again the enthusiasms, curiosity and excitement you felt then. You'll have your unforgettable memories of romantic meetings with lovely girls, of holding them close, whilst they discreetly lower their smiling eyes. Alternatively, the memories may be of girls not quite so modest, who provided you with a first taste of adult adventure...'

'I am sure you are right.'

Although all this was in French, the Revd John Mann gave it his close attention and seemed to agree.

'When I was your age, Mr Soames,' he interrupted, 'I came here, as to a City of Sin. You know about Sodom and Gomorrah? Looking back, I can't believe that I was capable of such daring and courage.' He said this smugly. 'But I was determined to discover for myself the nature of the enemy I'd dedicated my life to fight.'

'And did you?'

'Did I what?'

'Did you discover the nature of the enemy?'

'What enemy?'

It was apparent that despite his confidential manner and tremendous personal warmth, 'John', as he'd told me to call him, was only prepared to answer selected questions. When he didn't want to reply, he posed a series of catechisms, designed to evade and obscure. He didn't listen much to what people said to him. His role was to preach. It was for others to listen. At first this was confusing, but during the course of his week's Paris 'tour' it became depressingly familiar.

His first briefing, shortly after his arrival on the previous day had also been in the salon. He got his map of the city, meal times, programme of visits, and warnings about traffic on the wrong side of the road. Instead of being grateful, he'd been briefing me, pinning me into my chair, transfixing me with an Ancient Mariner's eye, washing me in a stream of reminiscence.

'... I soon got to know Paris well, and so I walked about all day, talking to everyone I met, asking them about their personal lives and their faith. I met all kinds of people, but I was mostly interested in helping the poor find their way to Our Lord. He supports them in their distress, you see. That is what I believed then.'

'What year was this?'

'Oh, dear me, it was a long time ago – after the Great War. Let me see, it was 1921 – no, I tell a lie, it was 1920. It was just before I married my dear wife, Clara. It was my first visit to France and it was new and strange to me. I was very excited about it all – at first that is – then I soon found my way around.'

'And you've come many times since?'

'After seeing Paris, I felt I'd had a powerful experience of the world apart from my parish. I was a simple curate then, you see. So I began to feel more settled. I'd just met Clara, my dear wife, and we wanted to get married and settle down, so I applied for my first living. It was outside Birmingham. Very suburban, it was, but Clara and I were happy there in the ways of the Lord. It was our first home, you see...'

It had been apparent at a glance that John was a clergyman, although he sported no 'dog-collar'. He was type cast as a bishop. Tall, lean dignified, with beaky nose and a fine head of bushy white hair, he appeared an exotic creature on the streets of the quartier, where heads turned, and eyebrows were raised as he purposefully strode along, puffing at his manly pipe and swinging his leather suitcase.

'What did you say?'

'Have you been here again since that first visit?'

'Would you like a fill of my tobacco? No? It's Erinmore. Good stuff.'

'I've grown out of a pipe.'

'What was I saying? Yes, well, we lived there for about five years, and left in 'seventeen, when father died. Because he never came with us to Liphook – no, wait – yes he did, because he helped me to put up the curtains in the vestry. He held one end, and then I was angry with him because he dropped it. What did you say?'

'Do you come often to Paris?'

'Certainly not. Only been once before, as a matter of fact.'

Although conversation with John was a one sided affair, he was undoubtedly an amiable, harmless old geezer, who needed only a listener with unlimited patience to make him happy. That was how he seemed on his first day. Distinguished in appearance, but undistinguished as a conversationalist. Soon, the details of his Birmingham, Liphook and succeeding parishes became only too familiar. And there were his stories of things going dreadfully wrong. The time when Clara spilt milk over the bishop in his purples. And the fearful occasion when he himself had offended, but, afterwards, the whole incident had been explained, and nobody had born malice. That he'd come to Paris in his youth was not mentioned again, nor that he had had in mind to recapture the past. When we met, he seemed unaware of the local life around him in the hotel and rue Victoire, more inclined to talk about England, home and beauty.

'The countryside of England – that's the thing. There's nowhere like it, you see, absolutely nowhere.'

'I believe parts of France are unspoiled.'

'It's pastoral, you see, that's the thing. When I look out of my study window I can see the Cotswold hills in the distance. Then, nearer, there's an apple orchard, and I can see sheep grazing. "Sheep may safely graze", eh? The whole scene is like an oil painting, beautifully composed.'

'Have you been to the Louvre yet?'

'Then there's the Cornish coast. All those little coves and inlets, with the sea rushing into them. And the windy headlands you can walk round...'

'They say that the Brittany coast is very like Cornwall.'

'And the Lake District is absolutely wonderful. You can see why Wordsworth enjoyed it so much. See it at a glance. Yes, it had a great influence on him:

"...One impulse from a vernal wood may teach you more
   of man

Of moral evil and of good than all the sages can..."

Yes, he was right, you know.'

It was tempting to tell him that since he seemed so blind to the attractions of Paris, he might have done better to take his holiday at home. Why he should have chosen to come on a WHIRLWIND Youth Tour was a mystery, but that was nothing to do with me. The boring old fellow was homesick. Tourists were sometimes like that. Amongst all the friendly little bistros of Paris, they yearned for their familiar pub. Anyway, he'd soon be back amongst the sheep and the apple orchards, and if Paris was making no impact on him why should that worry me?

After two or three days, it did. Considering myself a true if adopted Parisian, the need to sell the city to him became obsessive. How to make the silly old bugger aware there was an important world outside the Cotswolds, which he was missing. What piece of the magical jig-saw that was Paris would arouse his interest, hostility, attention, anything? A great church perhaps? That should break through his deadening complacency. Another group was due to visit Nôtre Dame, so it was easy to issue an invitation.

'You could join the morning tour, without extra cost, if you wish. Lunch is not included.'

'No, thank you kindly, I've got my plans made for the day.'

Where was he going? Each morning he had set off at a brisk pace, sucking at his disgusting pipe, haversack on back, Panama on head, ready for anything. Each evening, in reply to the polite question as to whether he had had a good day, he'd drone on relentlessly about his church in Broadway, the milkman's horse, which was friendly and fond of sugar, and the excellent cooking of his housekeeper, Mrs Goode. All this was sprinkled with references to the Way of the Lord and the True Path. It appeared his wife, Clara, had died many years ago – from overwhelming boredom, no doubt.

On the afternoon of the next day, when we were again sitting in the salon, Henri asked me: 'Have you read any of the works of Charles Fournier?'

'No, never.'

'Paris, you will understand, William, is a city of love, lust and passion, which prides itself on its capacity for logic and reasoning power.'

'I thought you regarded it as the City of Light.'

Henri was contemptuous of my English quibble.

'I have been thinking,' he said, 'about marriage. I have decided that I must love the woman with whom I shall spend my life.'

This was a timely decision because the next day, another act of Henri's matrimonial comedy was to be played out in the salon. In order to avoid interruption during his 'important meeting with all the parties involved', Henri asked me if, for one hour, I would kindly stand in for him at his reception desk and receive arriving hotel guests.

'Without hesitation!' I told him.

From this excellent vantage point I could see and hear all, particularly the four protagonists seated around the square central table, from which, in honour of this special occasion, the resident vase of crumbling paper dahlias had been removed. Henri's intended was dressed smartly for the occasion in a fashionable green silk outfit and a hat with a large brim. She wore a matching green necklace and brooch. She was tall and elegant and, when crossed, her legs displayed well shaped calves in sheer silk stockings. She carried on her lap a tiny King Charles spaniel, with a silver bell around his neck, reminding me of a Renoir painting. Undoubtedly, a merry widow with a certain style. Maman, for her part, had appeared in her customary shiny black sateen, but Henri had shaved specially for the occasion. He seemed less at ease than usual.

As they sat together, they conveyed the appearance of a foursome about to be dealt a hand of cards each. Maître Roustain had been allotted the role of dealer; the stakes were high, and the chime of the gilded mantelpiece clock signalled that play should begin. Predictably, it was to be a game in which all were losers.

'You will understand, Monsieur Henri,' the lawyer opened, 'that my client has been most reluctant to enter into any binding commitments until she has had the opportunity – the pleasure – of meeting you face to face. That will be accomplished today. You will be aware that is normally how these arrangements are conducted. My client wishes it to be understood that...'

'Oh, shut up, Antoine,' his client interrupted, 'and stop being pompous for a few seconds. What I want to say at the outset is that I'm not going to marry anyone until I've had an opportunity of spending some considerable time in his company – alone with him – so that we can together see whether we're suited to one another. If we're going to live together for the rest of our lives. Don't you all agree that that makes sense?'

She turned to Henri, who opened his mouth and then closed it. There was a moment of silent tension. Before Henri could speak, Maman got in her reply.

'Well, I can tell you here and now, Madame, that won't be

possible, because my son, Henri, hasn't got any time to be alone with anyone.'

'Really!'

'Ah, I think what Madame Rouget means by that remark is that . . . er, Monsieur Henri is normally engaged in the management of his enterprise, but I'm sure that he will make some time . . .'

'Normally, eh?'

For a while, the two ladies talked simultaneously to the lawyer, who looked helplessly from one to the other.

'Can't he speak for himself, or has the cat got his tongue?'

'If she wants to marry him she'll have to take him as he is, and if she doesn't like him then she doesn't need to marry him, does she?'

'Who does she think she is, telling me what to do? It's nothing to do with her whether I see him or not. He's a grown man, isn't he?'

'Certainly, Madame, but . . .'

'He's not as old as she is.'

'What a crumby place this hotel has become. No wonder they need money. It wants pulling down and rebuilding, if you ask me.'

'Nobody asked her, did they?'

This duologue continued for some time, in rising tones, with more and more calculated and insulting brutality. When, at last, they paused for breath, Maître R rose to his feet, turned and bowed stiffly to his host and hostess, and ushered his client into the hall. They whispered together for some time. Then he left Madame sitting on the dusty red velour couch and re-entered the salon. Now it was Maman's turn to get the benefit of his advice. Henri appeared neither to hear nor be interested.

When he'd got all three parties together, Maître R said unctuously 'We are all agreed that the best course of action would be to reflect for a period on what has been proposed. It is not easy to reach an immediate conclusion. Patience will be needed. Great patience! Undoubtedly this important alliance is capable of being

65

arranged in a variety of ways. All that can be said at this particular point in time is that we are all willing to carry the matter forward to a later meeting, which will give us time to reflect upon alternative strategies...'

'Nonsense!'

Recognising the inevitable, Maître R stood up, bowed, and ushered his expostulating client out of the salon and into the hall.

She told him graciously: 'Thank you for your help, cher Maître. I admire your patience and forbearing.'

'Not at all. Did you form a favourable impression of Monsieur Henri?'

'No impression at all yet. I'm sorry, but I have to go immediately, as my children will soon be home from school.'

'Ah, yes! Remind me what ages they are.'

'They are eleven and eight and they are the light of my life.'

'Of course. We will speak on the telephone because, despite the disappointments of today, I remain confident that we shall carry this matter forward.'

As soon as they'd gone, Henri came out into the hall, saying with admirable calm, 'Thank you for standing in for me. I am free now to return to my post, so you are released earlier than was expected.'

'Was your meeting a success?' I couldn't help asking.

Henri met my eye, hesitated for a few moments and said very calmly, 'It was a disaster and a triumph. At the critical moment I was unable to assert myself. But it was educative, enlarging my understanding of the way in which the human species has developed. But it was indeed a critical moment and I needed to stand up straight.'

'She seemed not an unattractive lady.'

'You are right. And the worst element is that I think I could have loved her. Why not? It would have been no hardship to have visited her in Room 7 as you once suggested. None at all. Certainly not! On the contrary! Whilst she was cuddling her dog, the idea of a trial night occurred to me as an agreeable opportunity lost for ever! But I have to tell you, my dear William...' Henri paused for quite a time. 'I have fallen hopelessly in love with another lady.'

'Are you prepared to tell me who that might be?' I asked, marshalling all my delicacy, diffidence and hesitation.

'You must have guessed: it is Madame Polianski. But I do not think she will ever return my love. What do you think?'

It was flattering to be consulted, but what could I say?

'Perhaps, when they come back here, you could invite her to dinner?'

'But I can't speak American, so I could never communicate my admiration for her.'

At this moment, Maman appeared in the hall. She glared at us both.

'You, Henri, you are a childish fool and you will regret all this. You, Monsieur,' she said, turning to me, 'have abused our hospitality. You are treacherous, duplicitous, villainous. All this is your fault. You should be ashamed of your conduct. You have no right to interfere in our lives. Typical of an Englishman, I suppose!'

Without waiting for a reply she stormed off.

Henri and I looked at one another, open-mouthed. I couldn't even ask her what I was supposed to have done. Or what he'd done. And my attempt at consolation was feeble.

'That's the way of the world, Henri. Let's go and have a drink!'

We sat silently in Bar Victoire for a few moments, each lost in his thoughts. Henri sipped his *vin blanc sec*.

Then he said, 'You know, William, any marriage at the present time would be a colossal disturbance to my existing way of life.'

'Do you think so?'

'As it is, I find it difficult to advance my medical studies and the intrusion of another person into the complex life of the Victoire would not have been easy to accommodate.'

'What about the repairs to the hotel?'

'Speaking confidentially, William, I believe there is no problem. Maman probably has all the necessary funds squirrelled away in her safe. It is just that she is always reluctant to consume our own money, and whenever the need arises she tries to apply someone else's. She is a very good financial manager, you see.'

'I see.'

After walking around all morning, I decided I'd go to Montmartre in the evening. I was glad to relax at noon on a sunny terrace nicely positioned for watching the girls go by. My lunch would be as it had always been – a baguette sandwich and a *pression*. But now I recognised that the girls – one of the eternal, dominating features of the Parisian landscape – had transformed themselves. All those perky berets, white blouses, swirling skirts and glossy stockings had disappeared. Now it was tee-shirts, jeans, and trainers. And they were much less clean and bright than the specimens stored in my memory bank. But behind the new fashions the famous beauties could still be identified. And the variety! My god, didn't they come in all shapes and sizes! You'd be spoiled for choice here. Maybe this was the local product I'd select from the marketplace to take back home as a gift-wrapped souvenir of my trip. Just at this moment I didn't have much sexual appetite, but later in the day perhaps ... after a bottle of wine, I might feel more inspired.

This cheering thought was destroyed by the surly waiter who short-changed me. There seemed to be a new harshness in Paris life.

Reluctantly, I did what I knew I had to do – wound up my courage and took a metro to Montparnasse. In the familiar train I allowed myself back into my uncertain, precarious present.

The train stopped at Montparnasse Bienvenue ... welcome! A good omen? I got out and stared up at the newly constructed tower. What a blight on my familiar landscape!

At the hospital, the receptionist was busy and I had to work hard to get her attention. 'It's a Monsieur Henri Rouget I'm looking for. A patient here, I've been told.' She consulted her screen and then disappeared for some minutes.

When she came back, she said, 'Are you perhaps, a relative?'

'No, I'm an old friend.'

'Please come this way.'

I followed her into a waiting room, but found it difficult to sit and relax.

After a few minutes, a tall elegant man of my own age came in, saying with conscious formality, 'I am Pontin, doctor and assistant director of this clinic. How can I be of assistance to you?'

'It's Monsieur Henri Rouget I've come to see. He is a patient here, so I've been informed.'

'Are you a member of his family?'

'No, I'm an old friend of his. From many years ago.'

A long pause.

'Well, is he here?'

'He was here. It is my duty to inform you that our friend died recently – yesterday in fact.'

'What ... what did he die of?'

'A malign and incurable intestinal tumour. Abnormal proliferation of cells. Please accept sincere condolences.'

'He died only yesterday?'

'Yes.'

I stood for some mute minutes looking at Dr Pontin, who stared back at me relentlessly. It seemed absurd that I'd arrived one day too late. Perhaps it had been some telepathic communication of Henri's fatal illness that had drawn me here.

Pontin said formally, 'I very much regret to be the bearer of such bad news.'

'It's not your fault,' I replied feebly.

'If you wish, Monsieur, you can meet with the widow of the deceased. You know her, perhaps? She is in our hospital today, making various funeral arrangements.'

I'd travelled several thousand miles to see my former friend, driven by affection and curiosity, and arrived in time for his funeral. The injustice of it brought tears to my eyes. I also felt a spasm of gastric pain, harbinger of my own death, soon or late.

'No, I don't. Wait! I mean yes, of course, I'd like to do that. Where is she?'

'I will request her to come and see you here. What's your name?'

'William Soames.'

'Wait here a few moments.'

I tried to collect my French vocabulary for a difficult encounter. Should I begin by offering sincere condolences, or explaining I'd known Henri before marriage?

Doctor Pontin reappeared and ushered in a small, thin, elderly woman, who said, 'I am Madame Ann-Marie Rouget. Who are you and what the bloody hell do you want, bothering me at this time?'

'I'm an old friend of your husband ... your late husband. From years ago. I came to see him. I'm very sorry if I'm imposing in any way...'

'Well, you're too late to see him. Henri's dead. Yesterday. What's your name?'

'William Soames.'

'Never heard of you.'

'I am from abroad and...'

'Obviously.'

Although all her former charms had disappeared, I'd recognised her at once. The fringe had gone but the slight squint in her eye was unmistakeable. A hundred possible questions crossed my mind. What I'd like to ask was whether Henri had continued his programme of sexual experimentation after their marriage, but that question would surely not be well received. I remembered my last conversation with Ann-Marie, when I'd promised to do some research for her. I failed to carry out that promise. Even

70

had I done so this would hardly be a good moment to claim the agreed reward. Nor to refer to their earlier acquaintance.

Instead, I said, 'Please accept sincere condolences. When is the funeral?'

'Tomorrow at eleven. Basilique Nôtre Dame de Victoires.'

'Thank you. I would like, if I may, to come.'

She barely nodded.

'Au revoir, monsieur.'

Outside, in the street, I remembered Henri once recounting how he'd first met her in 1940 when she'd been the mistress of a German general in the forces occupying Paris. After the Liberation of Paris in 1944, she'd been branded a 'horizontal collaborator'. I thought of going back and asking her to tell me about those events. Or saying to her: 'What was it like – your marriage with Henri? What happened to him? What kind of world did you and he jointly inhabit?' Or anything which would have offered some clue as to the manner of Henri's life and death. How and when had they come together in holy matrimony? Had they lived together in conjugal bliss at the Victoire? And what had Henri's terrible Maman thought about it? None of that would I ever know. If only I'd been able to think more quickly, I might have found words to break through her sour anger and transport us magically back to that past lost world. I went into a nearby café, sat at the bar, drank a cognac too quickly, and felt a gastric spasm, one which suddenly reminded me of the gut-wrenching Littletons. What an unmatched pain they'd been! How could I ever have forgotten the day I put on my travel-agent's arm-band, practised my welcoming smile – more of a rictus grin, it soon became – and set off for le Bourget airport: a journey through *les faubourgs* – a resonant phrase for territory at the margin of civilised life – a false city – the suburbs. At that time no high rise blocks, no factory belt, surrounded Paris.

The city of shabby, unpainted housing just stopped. Rural life, complete with cows, poplars and green fields just began. The square windows of the airport bus heightened this cinematic effect. Particularly when passing through a village complete with church, *urinoir* (green wrought iron), and peeling hoardings for Ricard and St Raphael. My destination: Le Bourget, to meet and greet a 'Special-One-Week-Air-Tour-Party', arriving in high style, luxury and sophistication by turbo prop direct from Croydon, England. Big spenders, these, from whom the sweet smell of money will waft upwards in dense clouds. They will buy wine in labelled bottles! Mr and Mrs Littleton from Fulham, rich enough to travel by air-liner, will disburse their way through shops and restaurants, benefiting from the savoir faire of their official tour guide.

They come through very late, long after all other passengers have disappeared. The first exchange extinguishes these expectations.

'Welcome to Paris!'

'One of our suitcases is missing.'

'My suitcase.'

'My wife's suitcase.'

'It's got all my things in.'

'They say it might come on another trolley.'

'We've been waiting for it.'

'Tell them they've got to find it immediately.'

An hour passes – a long period to radiate quiet reassurance, whilst at the same time engaging uniformed officials in urgent enquiry. They reply in detail.

'One wishes to apologise for the delay.'

'!'

'One can perceive that such delay can be disagreeable.'

'Indeed, very disagreeable.'

'One cannot supply a comprehensive explanation at the present time.'

'One possibility is that the suitcase might have been put on another baggage machine.'

'Or alternatively sent to another exit.'

'Or, one has to concede, it might have been put on another aircraft flying to another destination.'

'Undoubtedly, the error – that is, if there were one, and that is not yet admitted – occurred in England not here in Paris, but if one were to continue to be patient oneself, enquiries are being made, which, ultimately, one is supremely confident, will be successful.'

Whilst 'patienting' ourselves, these possibilities are recited to and discussed by the Littletons, Ernest and Edith, who, at this early stage, are relatively uncomplaining, dazed by a combination of two amazing events: having flown by aeroplane, and being in Paris ... almost.

Two hours pass. Then a dramatic development! Well, hardly. A deputation arrives, but they are merely inviting us to leave the address of our hotel so that the suitcase can be sent to us. There are, however, forms to be completed. On examination they seem to require a biography of each passenger, explanation of his financial and family circumstances together with a description of the missing object, together with a list of the items contained therein, showing where and when each had been purchased together with a statement of original cost prices and resale values as at a current date together with a formal declaration that everything stated above was true and correct in all respects. And there is a supplementary note to the effect that colour and weight of each item is to be indicated, together with (if known) the place of its manufacture. If the traveller compiling the report were to be suffering from any contagious diseases, these are to be enumerated in the space below. If the space below be found inadequate, a separate additional sheet of paper is to be used, but this should be carefully attached to the original form.

We wrestle with this dreadful document for some time, holding it against the wall in order to write. At first submission it is rejected as hopelessly incomplete, but finally it is accepted by an official with sufficient gold braid to satisfy Edith. Three hours have passed. We head for the airport bus, burdened only with one suitcase and a sense of dying hope.

At the Victoire, the whole story is told to Monsieur Henri,

who behaves impeccably. No downcast body gesture could have displayed deeper sympathy. However, telephoning to the airport brings little encouragement.

'One has been pursuing the possibility that it has been sent to Rome, Italy, but further investigation has proved this a false piste, and now, alas, one must wait until tomorrow as one is closing one's office.'

The Littletons retired early, without dinner, speechless and exhausted. It had been a tiring day for us all. After they'd gone, Henri expressed interest in Edith's nightwear arrangements.

He asked, 'Do you suppose, William, that if she sleeps in her skin that will be exciting for him?'

'He will feel that is appropriate in Paris.'

'She may wear one of his shirts.'

'That would not be big enough.'

'How will they resolve their problem?'

As Edith was substantially larger than Ernest in all apparent dimensions, borrowings seemed unlikely.

Next morning, they had both sufficiently recovered to demand early telephoning to the airport, which Monsieur Henri promptly and efficiently undertook. No news. Efforts were continuing. Patience was again counselled. This message was greeted with growing hostility. Mrs L was wearing her travelling oufit: blue woollen suit and pleated blouse, hopelessly hot and overdressed for the burning pavements of Paris. To keep her company, Mr L was also wearing his blue striped suit, waistcoat, school tie (Mill Hill?), watch chain, and carrying his brown trilby hat. He looked like a bookmaker's runner, sharp, and obedient to all instructions.

After *petit déjeuner*, they decided to go for a short walk. Edith led the way and Ernest followed through the swing doors, looking back at us reproachfully. He was in for a bad morning, but there was nothing we could do to help. Words of sympathy had already been proffered and rejected.

Henri said, 'Should we offer to assist her to buy some new lingerie?'

'I have not been requested to go on that delicate mission.'

'The English are too sensitive about such matters.'

'When she asks me to help, that will be time.'

During the day, which was hot and sunny, other matters intervened. In the afternoon, the Littletons were found in the salon, sitting stiffly in their chairs, alert for sound of the telephone. Each time it rang they peered across to Monsieur Henri at the reception desk who, each time, shook his head mournfully. They intercepted me in the hall.

'Mr Soames, what exactly are you doing about my wife's missing suitcase?'

'We're doing all we can, I'm afraid. We are telephoning the airport every hour. Is there anything else I can do to help?'

'What sort of thing?' (suspiciously)

'Well, would you like me to come with you to a department store, to make some essential replacement purchases?'

'Do you mean it's lost for good?'

'No, no, I'm sure it will be found soon. I meant replacement, until it is.'

'Who will pay for them? Will your firm pay?'

This was a predictable question, bound to cause more trouble. The office in London had already told me: 'You are on no account to accept any responsibility for the loss, as that will invalidate our tour insurance policy.' Nor was I to give any 'financial assistance', merely to express 'sincere regrets'.

'I can only offer my sincere regrets...'

'Regrets won't buy replacement clothes. There were all my best things in that case. There was my grey suit, quite new; green cocktail dress, two silk blouses, one with cream facings, and accessories...'

This list had been recited innumerable times, so that the temptation to complete it for her was almost irresistible.

'I'm not able to promise you compensation. That's for the company to say, but if you wanted to buy just a few things for immediate use...'

'You think I'll never get it back?'

'No, no!'

'This morning you said it might arrive at any time.'

'Yes, but...'

'Now you're saying it won't.'

'I don't know any more than you.'

'Well, you should know. You're the courier. It's your job to find my wife's case.'

'That's right, Ernest, tell him that it's his job.'

'Dinner is at 7.30 p.m.,' I said, to end the conversation. 'We meet here at about quarter past.'

They reappeared at the right time, wearing the same clothes and the same expression of aggrieved hostility.

Henri told them, 'I regret to have to inform you there is still no news of your missing suitcase, but efforts to find it are still continuing.'

He had repeated this sentence so many times that he could now produce it in perfect, natural English. If there were a million ways of expressing sorrow Henri would have attempted all of them. His whole posture spoke volumes of helpless regret. This manifest commitment was totally unappreciated.

News of the loss had spread amongst other tourist parties, whose words of concern were silenced by Edith's penetrating tones listing suitcase contents. More detail was now available, after a long afternoon's reflection. She had been wrong. The facings on her suit had been gold, and the lace on her nightdress was cream. The stockings were brand new, and the silver hair brush had been a present from an aunt who had died several years ago. This was fun for a while, but conversation soon reverted to the Eiffel tower trip arranged for that day. The Littletons refused to go. Whether they would visit the sewers of Paris on the following day depended on whether their suitcase arrived!

On yet another stuffy afternoon in the salon, Monsieur Henri recounted a critical episode from his past. Whilst my tourists diligently climbed the Eiffel tower, I had been reading *L'Education*

Sentimentale. The hero adores Madame Arnoux but, after inexplicable hesitation, rejects her in favour of her husband's mistress, Rosanette. What an idiot!

When Monsieur Henri came in, I paused in my reading, put a finger in my page and warned him: 'I have reached an exciting point in Frederic's life. He is making a decision. At last...' Henri was in reflective mood.

'Sometimes, my dear William, a critical fork in one's life occurs without intervention of any decision.'

'For example?'

'Well, for example, the death of my father was such an event. For five years, I had been happily pursuing clinical studies, terminated only when my father so inconsiderately died. His death was tragic but predictable. He fell not down, but up, the steps of the wine cellar. He was holding a bottle in each hand, lost his balance, and, with no hands to save himself, crashed fatally amongst the empties. Unfortunately, both bottles – St Emilion 1927 it was – were broken, so he expired in a pool of fine wine. Not an inappropriate death for a hotelier, although a lonely one. None of his guests was present. One dies alone – as Pascal says.'

'This somehow changed the course of your life?'

'On the same day, I lost my father, my vocation and my motivation. I argued against, but couldn't resist, my mother's insistence that I assume his responsibilities here. She is very strong-willed, my mother. But as you know, William, I haven't abandoned my calling altogether. Scrutinising the human body during a period whilst it is rejecting a disease can constitute a very satisfying form of scientific experiment.'

When embarked on his theories about homeopathy Henri tended to become boring.

'What year was this?'

'It was in 1937, just before the war.'

'Do you remember the Occupation of Paris and the subsequent Liberation by General de Gaulle?'

'Of course.'

Monsieur Henri stared into the distance for a few moments.

'In 1940, I first met my friend Ann-Marie. In the evenings, my clients, all senior German officers billeted here – stood in this salon, ordering champagne and cigars, and laughing loud and long at their own terrible jokes. Ann-Marie had been introduced on a commercial basis, to meet General von Studnitz, the Commander in Chief. He arrived with a flourish, monocle in place, chest aglow with medals. He sat where you are sitting and put his polished boots up on my best sofa. His HQ was at the Crillon but he came to his officers' billets here to maintain morale, they claimed. But it was to secure a supply of girls. He once told me: "Your city, Monsieur Henri, is famous for providing wine and women, both excellent commodities to victorious armies of the past. We are the victors now, and to the victors, the spoils of war." Then he bought everyone champagne. Ann-Marie was much taken by the Germans and they with her. Of course, in 1940, she was only, let me see, about seventeen and very inexperienced.'

'You knew her then?'

'Yes, of course. I watched her progress, because she was living in my hotel with an officer from General von Studnitz' staff – Major Braunich. They used to lie in bed together every afternoon, making love. As their bedroom was next to mine and they had both casement windows open, their conversation was agreeably titillating. Then she would order champagne, and I would take them up bottles and glasses, pour out and hand it to them as they sat up in bed. Twenty thousand francs a bottle!'

'Her German lover left her?'

'He left her because in 1941 he was posted to the Russian front. That was when Marshal Petain first instructed us to *collaborate* with the German authorities: a new locution which soon came into general use. It was an agreeable vacation for the Germans in Paris. Every day they told me they adored our city. Then Operation Barbarossa was announced. It was the twenty-fifth of June, the same date that Napoleon had chosen for his invasion of Russia. The officers here in the Victoire perceived their summer vacation was at an end.'

I put down my book. This story was more dramatic.

'Soon, Ann-Marie learned her German lover had been killed – by German shell fire apparently. I was saddened at his death. He was a very cultivated man who played his 'cello during the hours from five to seven. Bach, I think. I listened – in my own room, of course. His sense of rhythm was very strong. I preferred the sound of his 'cello to the sound of their bed springs.'

'Where were you during the liberation?'

'I was here. There was one day of conflicting rumours. Some said the Germans would fight to the last man, others that they would raze Paris to the ground. Some said that barricades had been thrown up in traditional revolutionary quarters, others that Seine bridges were being mined in preparation for wholesale demolition. There was a story about a German soldier who accidentally treads on a Frenchman's foot. Surprised, the Frenchman pushes the German slightly. Whilst they are apologising to each other, another Frenchman comes up and knocks the soldier to the ground. "Why did you do that?" he is asked. "Because I saw a Boche being pushed, so I thought the war was over,' he replies.

'You could hear in the streets the Marseillaise continuously played. "Le jour de gloire est arrivé!" Another more practical prophesy was "The Americans are coming!" But Paris wanted to liberate itself, to ensure that no one – least of all, Yankees – should share the honour and glory of such a famous French victory. The communists, you know, always find it helpful to punctuate their activity with dialectic as to the moral and philosophical basis of their actions. At that time the FTP had acquired a store of explosives, but they refused to hand them out, save to those comrades who were politically sound. Their status was to be tested by debate and rhetoric, which was difficult during the street fighting. Their commander expressed the view that Paris was worth two thousand dead. It is not clear why he chose that particular figure.

'All our neighbours in the *quartier* started to swim with the stream. The collabos, including the gendarmerie, put on FFI armbands, and then took them off again when the news changed. All the resistance groups, evoking the spirit of 1789, declared that they were in sole charge of this particular revolution. The next day, the exodus began. From the corner of rue Lafayette you could see traffic driving east. There were long lines of vehicles carrying the spoils of war back to Germany: antiques, sculptures, rolls of tapestries, food, weapons, anything of value. All Paris was watching them, mostly from their apartment windows. Some cheered, waved lavatory brushes and shouted that there was a load of shit flushing down the drain. The German officers billeted in my hotel finally departed after a four year vacation. My anxiety was that they didn't liberate the furnishings of my hotel. The billeting officer never paid their last month's bills.'

'What happened to Ann-Marie?'

He shrugged. 'She was convicted of *collaboration horizontale* and had her head shaved. She had a swastika painted on her breasts, and a sign saying "I have been sleeping with the Boches". Some collabos were insulted, others were beaten to death. It was a savage carnival from which I rescued her. She was standing under Pont Neuf shouting, "Listen, you bastards. I may have given my cunt to the Germans, but I've always given my heart to France. Always! Always!"

'Then she came back here but, because of Maman, I had to instal her at no. 122. Then the victorious Yankees arrived. Even the privates were rich enough to wear collars and ties! It was time to review my hotel room price list. The problem was delivering a high enough standard of service to satisfy them. They demanded baths every day – unheard of and drank "cocktails" at aperitif time. The practice of mixing different liquors together in one glass seemed extraordinary. Fortunately, their taste in girls was no different from that of armies of any other nationality. That was a facility I'd become accustomed to supplying for my guests – at short notice, if necessary – in bulk, night and day, in all requisite colours, shapes and sizes.'

Henri stared unseeing into the past and, for some time, I felt reluctant to drag him back to the present.

Then, in an effort to change the subject, I said helplessly, 'Do you think they'll ever find the Littletons' suitcase?'

Henri looked at me with contempt.

'Who knows?'

They never did. Throughout the whole holiday week, Edith wore her blue suit and Ernest wore his. Whether he'd brought other clothes and whether she made any purchases of underwear remained unknown. They did not leave the Victoire for long, so as to remain near the telephone, awaiting a message which never came. Henri continued to call the airport, but it had become a hollow ritual. On the last Saturday of their 'Special-One-Week-Paris-Air-Tour', when Edith had retired to rest, Ernest explained they had been looking forward to their holiday for a whole year.

'We had to make some savings out of my pay, but we thought it would be a big change from Torquay, where we've gone every summer since 1936.'

'I'm terribly sorry.'

'I know it's not your fault, but Edith gets cross when she's disappointed.'

'I can only offer sincere regrets that your holiday has been spoiled. But wouldn't the best thing be to forget about your suitcase and just enjoy your last evening in Paris? Would you like me to get you some tickets for the Opera? Tomorrow night they're playing *Simon Bolivar* and they bring real elephants onto the stage.'

'No thank you.'

The elephants were a well known dramatic feature. It was reported that after their appearance a stage-hand usually came on with a bucket to clear up their manure.

'What about the Folies Bergères, or some other typical show for your last night?'

'Edith wouldn't enjoy it. As you can see, she can't really think of anything else. I've tried to tell her that it doesn't matter that much.'

'I'll go round to Air France head office tomorrow and complain again.'

'It won't do any good,' he said despondently.

'They might give you some money. You must be entitled to compensation from the airline.'

'Edith wants to sue your tourist agency, but I know it's not your fault really.'

'I can only offer sincere regrets.'

On the following Sunday morning the problems of the Littletons were displaced by more exciting events.

Henri's working life normally began at 6.30 a.m., when he relieved the nightwatchman, and personally served *petit déjeuners.* Maman never surfaced until noon.

Throughout an arduous eighteen hour shift he remained at his post. Baggage was taken up and down, guests arrived and departed, regularly queuing at Reception to obtain keys, messages, bills and directions – and to deliver complaints. Henri's shift operated seven days a week, although Maman relieved him on Saturday evenings, when the hotel fell quiet.

Not much changed on Sundays, but Henri bathed and shaved in the morning after his strenuous Saturday night exertions at no. 122. This was when he was most relaxed, explaining the seductive charms of Ann-Marie in detail, using language which had enlarged my vocabulary well above first year under-graduate level. Thus it was astonishing, coming down late on Sunday morning, to find Reception desk unmanned, and guests clustered around it in a state of distress, angrily demanding their *café au lait.* Another lamentable failure on the part of hotel management! Something had to be done, but what? Banging on the door of Henri's bedroom brought no response. I peered inside at what looked like a deserted chemical laboratory, without sign of life.

Tapping repeatedly on the door of Maman's lair produced, after a long wait, an interrogative and angry 'Oui?'

'I'm extremely sorry to disturb you, Madame, but Monsieur Henri seems to be absent this morning. The *veilleur* has gone, and there is no one in charge of the desk.'

'Absent?'

'Well, I can't find him.'

'Who is that?'

'It's William Soames.'

'Who?'

'William Soames, the English tourist agent.'

'Go and bang on his bedroom door.'

'I've done that, and he's not there.'

'Nonsense!'

After some ten minutes of shouting through the door, Madame grasped the nature of the crisis and indicated that, as an unprecedented act of courtesy, and as a personal kindness to me, she would get up and attend to the business of her hotel.

'He must be at no. 122,' she added. 'Go and tell him he's wasted enough money for one night and if he doesn't return home immediately I'll personally come round and give him a good smacking.'

The purpose of establishments like no. 122, their personnel and clients are all familiar to any student acquainted with nineteenth century French literature. For example, there is de Maupassant's Madame Tellier, *la patronne* of a friendly house at Fécamp in Normandy. The locals go there most evenings, as if it were their club. She regularly takes her team for a day in the country, to get fresh air and fresh food, treating them with the loving kindness of an old Mum. On these occasions they romp around like school girls on a half-holiday. Madame Tellier confesses her sins, weeps in Church, and has the local judge as her earnest suitor.

But was reality like the literary version? At no. 122 all windows were shuttered; there was nothing to indicate commercial activity. The big door obviously led into a typical apartment building, constructed around a private courtyard. Eight bell pushes were grouped by the door, with eight names, any one of which could have been a code word for a house of ill-fame, brothel, whatever you like to call it. If I'd accepted Henri's cordial invitations to pass a convivial evening with him in this place (which he'd told me was like an English gentleman's club, where you met charming people, and had serious political discussions), I'd have known how to rescue him. Perhaps he'd had a political debate which had ended in a duel and he'd died an honourable death in the Bois de Boulogne. If, on the other hand, he'd been murdered for his wallet, they wouldn't have found much in it. He never had a centime left on Sunday mornings. The middle bell-push, which bore the label '*Mme de Passe*' seemed odds-on favourite. *Hôtel de passe* was an item of vocabulary which any student of the language knew meant brothel. The door clicked open with inviting smoothness, permitting me to climb the red carpeted stairs to the seventh floor. In turn, the apartment door was opened immediately by an impeccably turned out young maid: black ensemble plus white pinafore, nicely starched for Sunday morning, as was her tone of voice.

'Bonjour, Monsieur. Monsieur désire?'

'I'm looking for Monsieur Henri Rouget.'

'There is absolutely no one of that name at this address. Au revoir.'

'Wait. I'm from the Victoire, Monsieur Henri's hotel. He hasn't come back last night. I've been sent to look for him. It's serious.'

'Who are you looking for?'

'Monsieur Henri Rouget.'

'Wait a moment, Monsieur.'

Time passed, whilst a murmur of voices could be heard down the corridor, recapitulating what had been said. Then an ominous silence. Then a very large old creature appeared wearing a grotesque garment that could only be described as a peignoir, pink, translucent and trimmed with mink. She eyed me with unconcealed contempt and hostility.

'Who do you want?'

'Monsieur Henri Rouget from the Hôtel Victoire. He has disappeared.'

'Who sent you?'

'His mother.'

'That sour old hag. Tell her from me to disembowel herself with a pitchfork.'

'Certainly, Madame, but in the meantime is Monsieur Henri here?'

'*Attendez...*'

Waiting in the hall for a second time provided the opportunity to look around. It all seemed peaceful enough. There was absolutely nothing to confirm or deny that '*Mme de Passe*' had the coded meaning attributed to it. The apartment seemed to be decorated in a style which could be described as 'rich not gaudy', and was probably occupied by substantial and respectable members of the French bourgeoisie, who were doubtless summoning police to have me ejected and thrown into prison. I set myself to compose in French an eloquent declaration of innocence, coupled with an assurance that I was not an English spy, but a true friend of France.

All these speculations were interrupted by blood-curdling shrieks and screams from down the corridor. Heads appeared around doors, and were quickly withdrawn. Either my best French friend was being murdered whilst I waited, or else they'd just discovered his bleeding corpse. It was time for action. I ran down the corridor, pulling open doors, sticking my head round, and getting a variety of responses: yells, curses, grunts, invitations to climb back in as it was cold by oneself. Finally, I found him. In a tiny, darkened bedroom, smelling strongly of feet, grouped around a double brass bed, a whole collection of girls – old and young, fat and thin, of all shapes and sizes, blonde and dark, dressed and undressed, sufficient to satisfy the needs of a squadron of cavalry – stood screaming and wailing, as if the Day of Judgement had arrived. Dragging back the rich curtaining, I threw light onto the bed where lay Monsieur Henri, pale and still, cuddling his not-so-little beauty, Ann-Marie.

'They are dead, alas, but are they not beautiful?'

'Telephone immediately for the police.'

'And the ambulance service...'

'And the fire brigade...'

'Mon dieu, what a scandale for this house!'

'They have committed suicide together. He was always a romantic. I remember once he wanted me to go with him to the country.'

Pushing several hysterical girls out of the way, I struggled to seize his wrist, but succeeded only in finding Ann-Marie's. They both seemed very warm; if the Grim Reaper had reaped them it must have been very recently. As if to confirm the theory of a suicide pact, there were two glasses on the bedside cabinet, from which they'd obviously drunk before retiring for a night of bliss. The girls crowded round, pushing me back. I jostled for position.

Outside no. 122, the hee-haw sound of police or fire engine sirens could be heard getting louder. One telephone call had been enough to alert the public services of Paris. A tremendous banging on the door preceded the ferocious entry of a police riot squad, wearing white helmets and gloves, carrying sub-machine guns, closely followed by two firemen with drawn axes, and a man in a white coat.

This last individual announced formally: 'Will all ladies and gentlemen present in this bed-chamber please do me the courtesy of standing back? I am the area duty medical officer and, in accordance with the powers vested in me, I now request that all persons please co-operate so that I may inspect the cadavers, so that I can carry out the necessary and proper procedures respectively authorised under the Law of fourteenth April 1937.'

In the rush to retreat I was pushed to the ground, and a girl trod on my hand. Policemen, firemen and girls jostled angrily for position. This was a dramatic death-bed scene no one wanted to miss. The room had become so crowded that one of the prettiest (and most undressed) girls gave an especially loud scream and toppled across the bed in a classical swoon. Unfortunately, she failed to position herself correctly, hit the bed side on, and rolled onto the floor. Firemen and gendarmes gallantly bent to retrieve her, dropping their machine guns on the bed so as to have both hands free for recuperative massage. That was a mistake. Safety catches had been taken off, so as to be prepared for all contingencies. A short burst of automatic sub-machine fire shattered the windows, and those not already on the floor dived for it. Anyone who had not been screaming before now screamed. The Day of Last Judgement was at hand. Soon the incident would disintegrate into a traditional Parisian crisis, involving armed gendarmerie, shooting, screaming and tear gas. In that period, such events could soon escalate: barricades would be thrown up in Boulevard St Michel red flags waved, stretchers would carry away wounded, the coalition government would fall, the franc collapse, foreign policies would be reversed...

But a sobering element was to hand. In response to the gunfire and hysteria within, the municipal firemen in the street outside, who had already mounted their hoses, now, in accordance with their standing instructions, directed a stream of icy water through the broken window. Called out early on a Sunday morning, they were determined their rescue mission should not be in vain. This jet hit the recumbent Henri full in the face and splashed over bed and surrounding spectators, all of whom screamed with renewed ferocity.

'*Merde, alors!*'

Abruptly, Henri threw back the covers, and staggered out of bed, wiping water from his face. Ann-Marie also came to life and bolted like a rabbit for the door, scuttling between police and girls with a skill born of many such experiences.

'What in god's name,' asked Henri, quite mildly, 'is going on here?'

Considering his nakedness and wetness, he bore himself with considerable dignity.

'It's late. Maman sent me to collect you. We were worried.'

'What time is it?'

'Nine-thirty, almost.'

'Mon dieu! That is serious.'

Ignoring the assembled multitudes, he began to hunt around the disordered bedroom for clothes.

This seemed the right time to retreat before responsibility for these *événements* was allocated. Moreover, it suddenly seemed urgent to assure Maman that her beloved only son had been found safe and well, and would be home shortly. And to find some dry clothes. Maman received the good news with ill grace.

Later in the day, feeling that some explanation was due, I said to him 'You must have had a lot to drink last night.'

'No, not at all. Very little in point of fact.'

'You seemed to be knocked-out.'

'I had been experimenting with a new herbal potion. It is designed to increase sexual gratification. Both Ann-Marie and I took a substantial dose. It is not unpleasant to taste, being constructed principally from the flowers of the forest.'

'Did you explain that to the police and the firemen.'

'Certainly. The officer in charge was most interested, and asked for a specimen to test it out for himself.'

'I thought they'd carry you off to the Bastille.'

'Mon cher William, the Bastille was pulled down in 1789, as you well know. But you are right. They were inclined to be very angry with me at first, claiming that it had been a false alarm, and that I would have to bear the cost.'

'How did you pacify them?'

'There was very little I could say, apart from offering my sincere apologies for inadvertently causing them so much trouble.'

'And that satisfied them?'

'Not entirely, but Madame offered them all a free night at no. 122 provided they forgot about the whole incident. She hates publicity, you see. It's so bad for her reputation. Well, as you can imagine, that was an offer which none of them could refuse.'

'Wasn't she angry with you?'

'She was at first, but she thinks she will attract new business, and it is advantageous for her to have clients who work in the public services.'

'And is Ann-Marie OK?'

'It must have been an interesting experience for her, and I'm looking forward to hearing her describe her physiological sensations next Saturday.'

Henri went up to his room, came back and handed me an old and tattered notebook.

'William, I think you would be interested to read these few pages.'

I sat in the salon and read.

9 SEPTEMBER 1944

Yesterday evening, old Monsieur Robert appeared early, looking unusually pleased with life. He was anxious to discuss with me this week's current ideologies.

'Have you seen, Monsieur Henri, today's Figaro? It contains a newly published Manifesto of the National Committee of French Writers, and it is signed by three members of the Academie Française – Georges Duhamel, François Mauriac, plus Camus, Eluard, Queneau and Sartre.'

He pushed the paper under my nose, which irritated me.

'Look, it concludes with this stirring message:

'Let us remain united in Victory and Freedom as we were in Sorrow and Oppression. Let us remain united for the Resurrection of France and the fair punishment of imposters and traitors.'

I told him: 'Alas, Monsieur Robert, I have to confess my lack of commitment to great issues. In that matter, I am dégagé. As an hotelier, I cannot pick and choose who I receive as guests. I am obliged to maintain a neutral stance towards their behaviour. Whatever their nationalities, their follies and absurdities, it is for me to nod and smile graciously. So is it also for me on the larger political stage.'

'But Monsieur Henri, these are issues which affect us all.'

'So you say, Monsieur Robert. In my view, great leaders, promoting great new causes come and go with remarkable speed. Just like my clients. Here today, gone tomorrow. When they are in office, they are in power, and their ideas circulate. When they have gone, we forget about them. They may reappear, and they may not.'

'You are a great pragmatist, Monsieur Henri, but you cannot turn your back on history.'

'And I am not in favour of the punishment of "traitors". The patriots of today were the traitors of yesterday ... and vice versa.'

'Monsieur Henri...'

'Look at this fellow Charles De Gaulle. Last week, he was a traitor, a Pretender to the throne, a refugee in exile, with a price on his head. Today, he is a great hero and a great leader. When he appears in procession, we all cheer.'

'Monsieur Henri, you are a cynic as well as a pragmatist.'

Maybe Robert is right. But being a hotelier destroys one's capacities to believe in causes. That is one reason why I would like to give it up. The only real issue is whether the clients will pay the bill, and my new Yankee guests seem very promising in that respect. But they are like all the armies of the world. Drink and fornication are their principal activities. They are busily liberating the brothels and the wine cellars of Paris. You would think their war was over.

The possibility of abandoning my life as an hotelier and pursuing my true vocation seems to come a little closer this week. My mother is grievously ill. When I found her slumped at her desk, she appeared to be counting the week's takings, but actually was in a state of collapse. At first, not realising this, I said, 'If it has been a good week, Mama, I should be grateful for an advance of ten thousand.'

There was no reply. Then, seeing her contorted features, I shouted to her: 'Mama, Mama, it's your son, Henri!'

Still no reply. A heart attack, I thought, from which it seemed she might not recover. She was carried to her room, and confined to bed. *During her illness, I naturally took the opportunity to possess myself of her keys. Had she been conscious she wouldn't have surrendered them. Last night, I opened the safe in her office and was amazed at the total amount of money which she'd over the years squirrelled away. Nearly ten million francs! Of my money – well, if you like, our money. I shall make some preliminary enquiries about buying, a chaumière in the country, perhaps the valley of the Loire, and I shall try to find a possible purchaser for the Victoire. If Mama recovers, she will be presented with a fait accomplit. Moving to the country will be beneficial for her health. Of course, if she dies, there will be no problem. Naturally, I am anxious about her, and look forward to her full recovery. On the other hand, I do confess that her death would solve many problems. She does not seem to enjoy life as a widow with an unsatisfactory son, and has no interests in life other than counting the hotel money. So, apparently, death would not be a great deprivation for her.*

On Saturday I went as usual to visit my friend Ann-Marie, who is now permanently installed at no. 122. She was sitting immobile staring out of the window into the place below. I could see that she is reliving what was, undoubtedly, a terrible experience for her. Let's hope that she's slowly recovering from it. Her fine blonde hair is beginning to grow again, and her bruises are fading. Let's hope she is using the efficacious ointment I have given her. It's difficult to distract her, or engage her attention, and my plans haven't seemed of much interest to her. I told her: 'If I am able to move to the country, madamoiselle, I would like you to accompany me. It would be the start of a new life together for us. You could be of great assistance to me in the medical practice I intend to establish. Would you like that?'

'I don't know.'

'We will find a petite chaumière, and live simply but happily. I have not decided precisely where to go. At present, I favour the region of the Loire, perhaps Tours, which was my birthplace. The countryside is very attractive and good French is spoken in that area. Around the river banks there are beneficial herbs growing in great abundance. What is your preference?'

'I don't know.'

She has lost much of her vivacity, but that is understandable in the circumstances. I have thought of inviting her to move in with me to the Victoire, but there are two problems. Firstly, my mother may recover, and she would never tolerate her presence. Indeed, she is hostile to any friend of mine, but she would absolutely condemn Ann-Marie as a *collaberateuse horizontale*. Then there would be terrible scenes, with shouting and screaming, which I deplore. It is so bad for the reputation of the hotel. And then also there are the Yankees. So I have decided to leave her at no. 122 for the present. She is comfortable there, and not too many demands are being made on her.

In order to help her recovery, I have encouraged her to tell me her life story. As you might expect, she is torn with guilt. About many different elements in her past life. After many false starts, and with much hesitation, she said: 'Did you know I have a son, Etienne, now aged two? I haven't seen him since he was a tiny baby. Now they tell me he's been ill with scarlatina. At death's door. I should have been with him. Why wasn't I?'

'How ill is he?' I asked, my professional interest being aroused.

'His grandmother says he is getting better.'

'It's the war that has disturbed all our lives.'

'Not yours.'

I thought it best to ignore that. Anyway, it's true. The irony is that I would have liked my life to have been changed and am now struggling to change it.

Apparently, Etienne has been living with Ann Marie's mother-in-law, but now is with his father – not her husband, Albert, whom I've met – but another type. He is taking care of him. So I told her: 'You have nothing to reproach yourself for. Your son has survived even without your care. You are very lucky. I would like to have a son.'

'I don't want children.'

I'd never thought much about having children before, but suddenly the idea of it interested me. Perhaps, when we are settled in the country, far from the horrors she had endured in Paris, she might think differently. After all, she is very young, and I believe a better diet of fresh country food would aid her return to normality.

I said to her: 'Do you think you are ready yet for a full medical examination?'

'Go away.'

What she really said was 'Fuck off!' She can be very brutal, but that is understandable. As it happens, my enthusiasm has been greatly stimulated recently, perhaps by the liberation of the city, perhaps by my American guests, who have been explaining to me the way things are done in their country. Being in funds, it has seemed there is no problem, and the personnel at no. 122 have recently been reinforced with some interesting new recruits.

When I returned to the hotel on Sunday morning, I found that my mother was conscious and asking for me. To be more precise she was asking for her keys. She seems to have made a rapid recovery from her attack, apparently of a gastric nature. My diagnosis was erroneous. And the plans which I was hopefully and busily making during the short period of her illness now seem unlikely to come to fruition. Frankly, I am disappointed.

I gave Henri back his diary.

'What a very sad story!'

'Yes.'

Later in the day, I decided to experience again an old fashioned evening of so called 'gaiety and pleasure'. That's what my tourists had been so generously offered -- on the last evening of each tour -- and that would surely help recapture the exciting, sparkling city I'd once known and loved. After an early dinner, I took a metro to Place Pigalle, sat in a café and drank a large cognac rather too quickly. Now there were crowds of beggars on the street, some playing accordions, others eyeing passers-by with undoubted menace. The Paris homeless lay around the metro exit, wrapped in dirty blankets, giving off foul odours and extending their hands. Most had bottles of wine by their side, and all were smoking. None of the crowds around me seemed to be speaking French: mostly German and Arabic. Surreptitiously, I moved my wallet into a hip pocket and buttoned the flap. Then I had another large cognac and felt better ... then worse...

Boulevard de Clichy was very different from how I recalled it. The famous police station, about which stories were told, had disappeared. Henry Miller had claimed that, for a dare, he'd gone into it shouting, 'Shits! You're a crazy bunch of shits!'

The policemen all looked at him for a moment, then at each other, then shook their heads, remarking, 'Fucking stupid foreigners!'

Then they went quietly back to their demanding paper work. A story which didn't seem quite so funny, now. Anyway, Miller's stories were all outrageous – another way of saying 'fictitious'. He'd claimed to enjoy the world of Pigalle because the night life there was 'colourful', scandalous, wildly erotic. That was what had sold his books. Actually, he'd stayed in his apartment all night, scribbling.

Now the welcoming restaurants he'd described had become sex-shops. I went into one and looked at lavishly coloured photographs of couples relentlessly coupling. The anatomical detail was repellent. The erotic effect was zero – minus zero! It didn't give me the slightest urge to stick my dick – which I still greatly treasured – up one of those orifices. I might never get it out again. With this predicament in mind, I felt carefully, to make sure it was still there, then went into yet another noisy and crowded café, stood at the counter and drank yet another cognac.

A black man sidled up to me saying, 'Are you lonely, Mister?'

I bolted for the door. Then I walked as slowly as I dared, and a bit unsteadily, to Metro Anvers and took the funicular to Sacré Coeur. Japanese tourists sat in groups on the steps of the basilique shouting and singing, as street traders passed amongst them, trying to sell ugly African carved heads and disgusting plastic models of the Eiffel tower. Pushing through jostling crowds,

I got to Place du Tertre. The ghosts of Dufy and Matisse were still there – I could see them through my alcoholic mist. No, wrong! They'd all gone, but there was no shortage of living painters in the square, selling their clear, brightly coloured products at negotiable prices in all known languages.

It vaguely occurred to me that this was where J-P, according to his many times told tale, had found his lovely American girl. His perfect romance. And where he'd confessed his ambition to become a great doctor, rich and famous. A great doctor! It struck me like a punch in my queasy gut. The doctor in the clinic was J-P! I'd forgotten his surname was Pontin. Jean-Paul Pontin. Or was it Jean-Philippe? 'Who cares?' I thought. J-P probably stood for Jaundiced-Prick. Or Javeline-Propre? Everyone had called him J-P. He'd been Henri's friend. The fact that he'd said Henri was *our* friend, not *your* friend, had escaped me at the time, but was now explained. So he'd finally passed his exams, and fulfilled his ambition to be a 'great' doctor...

Meeting J-P and Ann-Marie together was, I realised, through my drunken stupor, not an extraordinary coincidence, but a natural consequence of my search for Henri. It was, in retrospect, predictable that Henri should have finally selected Ann-Marie as his week day – as well as Saturday night time – partner, although, at the time, the idea would have seemed laughable. That she'd become a not-so-very-merry-widow was equally predictable. Her professional career at no. 122 had seemed normal at the time, but from present perspectives it seemed to have been a monstrous way of life. Surely marriage to Henri had been better than that. Neither J-P nor I had recognised one another, but after thirty years that wasn't surprising. He hadn't remembered my name, but then I hadn't remembered J-P's. I began to reconstruct my former version of Henri's death. At his bedside had been two lifelong playmates, who'd respectively become wife and doctor. Had that made his final passage easier or more difficult? How was I to know what his death was like? How was I to know whether he'd really died? Why had I drunk so much cognac?

What the fuck was going on? What was I supposed to be doing here? Where was I anyway?

Suddenly, I began to feel ill. The gastric discomfort increased in intensity, became quite bright and rose in my chest. I could feel the cold sweat on my forehead and desperate choking sensations in the throat. Waves of simple terror swept over me. This was it, I thought. Place du Tertre was to become my last view of the world. Soon, I'd satisfy my wish to meet again my friend Henri, who'd got to the after life – assuming there was one – ahead of me by only one day. Our rendez-vous would have been arranged to occur in the marble pillared hall of Hôtel Victoire, where Henri, unshaven, but wearing his silver tie, would be standing at reception, ready to check me in, and bow me into the lift, which would carry me rattling up to rest in no. 9 (a superior single room, complete with washbasin and bidet) throughout All Eternity. The Victoire would be peopled with phantom guests, all searching for the bathroom, or waiting for the *petit déjeuners* that never came.

Leaning against a wall, I told myself that the spasm was passing. This was a small foretaste of what was to come. Death in pain, isolation and indignity. Or was I suffering merely acute indigestion induced by rich food and wine? It might have been the lobster I'd had for dinner, agitated by grisly images of cancerous intestines and inflated multi-coloured sexual organs. A second spasm gripped me. I looked around for a convenient place to vomit, and only just reached the gutter. German tourists in *lederhosen* jumped away to avoid being splashed, but otherwise passers-by took not the slightest notice. I stood for a moment regaining breath and wiping my mouth. For the moment, the pain had subsided. Normality began to reassert itself. At first, I imagined that my bowels might have voided themselves into my pants, but when I found that I hadn't suffered that final indignity I began to feel better. Unwilling to examine the terrifying multi-coloured substances regurgitated, I walked unsteadily round the square, hoping to find somewhere I could lie down briefly. It appeared that, for the present, the finger of Death had passed me by, but how long might I have left? I took a taxi back to the Georges V and fell into bed.

Now it was Monday, a bright sunny day full of promise. That was because the Littletons were finally due to depart. Their lonely suitcase had been brought down into the hall, where it stood as if in continual reproach. They had no other packages, so had apparently purchased nothing in Paris. Edith had ceased to speak to me directly; we communicated through Ernest or Henri. They had hired a taxi to take them back to Le Bourget, and insisted that the tour agency should pay.

Predictably, angry letters of complaint and international law suits lay ahead. Apart from the financial claims, the local courier (me) would stand accused of (a) having done little or nothing to assist the clients in their difficulty and distress and, in addition, of (b) sexually assaulting Mrs Littleton and, in addition, of (c) making public reference to her bodily odours. These last charges, conveyed to me by Henri, and undoubtedly of his own invention, set me laughing aloud, just as they appeared for the last time, glaring and tight lipped. As there was nothing at all that could be said, we waited together in silent and reciprocal loathing for a taxi to arrive. So began one of those intervals of time when clocks stand still and the angry, exhausted world falls quiet. Paralysis descended on the city of Paris as we looked at our watches, concerned in our different ways as to whether the taxi would be late, how long it would take to get them to Le Bourget what other possible catastrophes could occur further to destroy (if that were possible!) an innocent couple's one and only Paris holiday.

The sullen silence was penetrated by the sound of not one but two taxis, simultaneously braking outside the Victoire. All taxis in Paris were black Renault *traction avant*, so the effect was of double vision. Both drivers came into the hotel together. The first said that he had come to conduct two persons to the airport at Le Bourget. The second said he had come to bring this missing suitcase, with which he had been entrusted by the airport authorities. We pushed the Littletons *and* their suitcase into the first taxi, and waved them good bye.

It proved to be another hot midsummer day. After a liquid lunch, celebrating the Littletons' departure, I stumbled back into the dusty salon of the Victoire, where the air was thick with fumes of Gauloises, and curtains were drawn against bright August sunshine. My tourists were nowhere to be seen – limp in the Tuileries perhaps. In his niche outside the hotel, Emperor Napoleon had fainted from thirst and heat. Maman could be seen sleeping in her chair, mouth open, hand clutching the bunch of keys she wore at her waist.

In the salon, despite the temperature, strident debate was in progress. Powerful arguments were being advanced and refuted. Clearly Monsieur Henri and Jean-Pierre had lunched on numerous *coups de blanc* at Bar Victoire. Fred had arrived in the early afternoon, from some mysterious rendez-vous, carrying a square package wrapped in brown paper. An Old Master, no doubt. Was he buying or selling? From the gleam in his eye a significant deal had been done. Thus all fortified, they were launched on Love and Women, those elements in Life which move into sharper focus as the bottles empty. Interrupting dreams of my own lost Jacqueline (would I ever find her again?), Henri continued.

'Love does not make lovers happy. It cannot do so. That is a tired illusion which romantic novelists have encouraged. On the contrary, love makes one wretched and miserable, for it is, by definition, a state of longing for the unattainable, or, at least, what is not yet attained.'

'I comprehensively disagree.'

'Kindly wait for me to conclude my thesis. The act of love, complete with sexual fulfilment, on the other hand, represents a delightful sensation of apotheosis and release. These two human experiences are often confused, but they are truly separate and distinct.'

'But the former may lead to the latter.'

'That is not an inevitable consequence.'

'And may improve the pleasurable quality of the latter.'

'I concede that to be possible, but not necessarily. Indeed, a sense of admiration for a lovely girl may inhibit one from pulling her knickers down, thus diminishing, rather than increasing, pleasure.'

'That is not my experience,' said J-P. 'On the contrary, passionate love can be essential as a prerequisite for screwing. To do as you propose, mon cher Henri, to screw simply for the physical sensation, is to go for one dimension only. It is an oversimplification of a complex human procedure.'

'Then what is your advice about my proposed marriage?'

J-P adopted a professional tone.

'According to my diagnosis, mon cher Henri, the intended bride is, and always has been, incapable of producing children. To that extent it would be a disappointing union.'

'How can you know that?'

'I have made it my business to see her – albeit from some distance – and I am telling you that her incapacity is apparent from her bone structure.'

'What has bone structure to do with it?'

'A great deal. No matter if you were to fuck night and day for a week it would be to no avail.'

'I find that difficult to accept. I have not got your training, J-P, but I know that fertility and bone structure are not related elements.'

'Believe me, Henri, I am putting my professional knowledge at your disposal.'

'I have to concede that Maman would be terribly disappointed at not getting any grandchildren.'

Whilst this conversation had been going on, I sat silent looking from one to the other.

'And I too,' Henri added thoughtfully, 'would like the family line to continue. Children would be part of my life when I retire to the country.'

'Well, there you are,' J-P said with finality. 'You're not betraying anyone by not going forward with this sterile marriage.'

'J-P, you must tell Maman what you've told me. That would be a great help to us both. After all, you're a doctor – or soon will be.'

'She wouldn't believe me. She hates me. Why don't you tell her?

'She wouldn't believe me either,' Henri replied sadly. 'Sometimes, I think she hates me – hates everyone.'

'You mustn't, Henri, let your life be ruled by her. You know how much I admire your way of life and value your friendship. I am telling you these facts to help you.'

All this extraordinary dialogue left me torn between laughter and despair. I remembered that the lovely lady had told her notary that she had children aged seven and eleven, and that she had to get home before they came back from school. They always wanted their dinner then. So, as far as past capacity was concerned, J-P was comprehensively wrong. As to the future, he might be right. Was he culpably wrong, or just being pompous? Should I tell them what I knew? What I had secretly overheard? I could hardly do that. Surely my contribution would be inconclusive and unhelpful. J-P had told Henri what Henri wanted to hear. It hardly mattered whether it was true or false. Why spoil it all?

I reflected instead, for the millionth time, how in Paris one could sit for hours theorising about sex. In a companiable group in England they might have discussed the football results or the price of beer. They turned to me with friendly curiosity.

'What, William, is your view of this problem?'

'I am insufficiently experienced to form a judgement.'

'But that is terrible!'

'My dear friend, we must assist you, without delay. Henri, we must advance his sentimental education: we must provide William with the opportunity for an encounter which will be of lasting value to him. It will help him with his studies when he returns to England. It is useless his spending his time reading about Héloise and Abelard, and all the great love affairs of the past, until he has done it regularly himself, preferably in a well-equipped apartment, where he will succumb to the wildest passions and, ultimately, only after a long period of anticipation, consummate his love.'

'I have already invited him to accompany me on a visit to no. 122.'

'That is not what William needs at all. He will get a nasty complaint, and his little English prick will wither and drop off.'

'What experience do you suggest?'

'He must meet a *jeune et jolie française*. I will introduce him into a bourgeois family with three beautiful daughters. He will be much admired by all three because he is English, and he has excellent manners. He will choose amongst them, and establish a relationship. Later, they may set up in an apartment.'

'But I have no money.'

'Of course not. If you had money, you would not be staying at the Victoire.'

The logic of this was irrefutable. As there was no more to drink, the party soon broke up, and the promised introduction seemed forgotten. But a few days later, J-P descended on me, as I was reading *L'Education Sentimentale*. Frederic had just begun his ambivalent relationship with Madame Arnoux.

'William, I bring good news!' J-P shouted. 'We are invited to dine chez les Dubois. I have told them about your problem.'

'What problem?'

'That you are in need of a sentimental education, of course. Madame expressed herself as enchanted to entertain a well-bred young Englishman who is my friend.'

'How exactly did you explain my "problem"?'

J-P ignored that.

'You are to wear a different shirt,' he said, examining me for

101

the first time. 'One that does not smell as much as the one you are wearing today. And a tie. Do you have a club tie?'

'I don't have a club.'

'It is not important.'

It was agreed that J-P would fix a date for this magnificent occasion and would let me know.

In the meantime, there was a day tour to the palace of Versailles to be organised.

'Once in a life time,' the tour brochure claimed, 'it is the destiny of all travellers to make pilgrimage to Versailles, palace of extravagance, luxury and pleasure. Building work – lasting 42 years at a cost of 82 million *livres* – continued throughout the long life of The Sun King – Louis XIV, a monarch with many enthusiasms: architecture, hunting, music and lovely girls.'

This was a whole-day excursion – with complimentary picnic lunch included in the 'One-Week-Whirlwind-Youth-Paris-Glamour-Tour'. We were accompanied by an expert multi-lingual guide, supplied by the coach hire company, without extra charge. He turned out to be a stooping, scholarly fellow, who formally introduced himself as 'Monsieur Théophile Chaulieu, Professional Historian and Multi-lingual Tourist Guide', a long and awkward declaration, which he had to repeat some twenty times whilst shaking hands with each member of my party. It was important, he whispered to me, to establish personal relationships with clients, because that encouraged them when, at the end of a guided tour, it came to the important moment for *pourboires*. These, he confided, were his only source of income. His elaborate introduction ritual delayed our start by thirty minutes.

We also took with us ten fresh baguettes, smoked ham, three kinds of cheeses (Camembert, Brie, and Saint Paulin, all from Normandy), fat tomatoes from Provence, melons from Cavaillon, bottles of mineral water, both *gazeuse* and *non-gazeuse*, promising ourselves a delicious picnic lunch in the elaborate gardens of the palace.

During our coach journey, Monsieur Théophile kept us

entertained with exciting tales of earlier visitors, who'd made pilgrimages to Versailles.

'It was on Sunday 5th October 1789,' he said, 'the starving women of Paris, some of doubtful repute, tramped twenty kilometres along muddy roads in the driving rain and forced their way into the château, demanding that Louis XVI provide (not baguettes for a sunny picnic in the parc) but enough bread for all Paris.'

We didn't find it difficult to imagine the mood of that mob.

'By the time they got there,' he explained, 'they'd naturally become resentful, angry and confused.'

So were we. Our coach had arrived late at the hotel to collect us, and the driver twice lost his way in country lanes leading to the town. Moreover, some 160 years later, it was still raining heavily.

When the ladies of Paris got to the gates, shouting their immediate needs – 'We want bread!' – they were officially welcomed by palace dignitaries, who placated them with wine and speeches. Then, drenched with rain, they forced their way into the *Salle des Menus Plaisirs* – an indoor games room, used for bingo, or whatever the equivalent then. Louis had agreed to see a deputation, and a seventeen-year-old flower girl, beautiful and virtuous was selected as spokesperson. Overcome with awe at the solemnity of it all, she collapsed at Louis' feet. The king took her into a convenient alcove and gave her a quick cuddle to revive her. The onlookers cheered, and a dangerous confrontation was avoided. Then the National Guard arrived, shooting at sight. A fresh armed mob burst into the Palace, charged up the Royal Staircase, murdered sentries and headed for the Royal Bedrooms. Marie Antoinette ran barefoot down one secret passage way into the King's bedroom whilst, from sheer force of habit, he ran down another into hers. The next day both of them were brought as prisoners to Paris. They never saw Versailles again. Their destiny was with the guillotine.

Moved by this long and chilling tale, we climbed stiffly from our bus at the Place d'Armes, reflecting on our own immediate needs. Only after satisfying them were we able to contemplate the historic vista before us. How pathetic seemed these last vestiges of an ancient regime, in transition from wealth and power to humiliation, cruelty and death! Further philosophical reflections had to be postponed, whilst we galloped half a mile through the drenching rain to the entrance of the Royal Palace. All we needed to reconstitute the events of history was the trumpet's rallying call and a command to draw sabres. Monsieur Théophile did his best. He'd taken the precaution of bringing a long raincoat, which flowed out behind him. As he led his troop forward in a great, sweeping cavalry charge, he shouted encouragement and waved his umbrella.

At the entrance, we joined a long queue of American ladies and gentlemen, twittering like birds and taking one another's pictures. We stood with them (in the driving rain), whilst our multi-lingual guide disappeared (in the driving rain) to see about tickets. Time passed. We got wetter, but after twenty minutes (in the driving rain), we could not get wetter still, because we had become wettest. In order to placate my tourists, now muttering about pneumonia, I set off to track down our Monsieur Théophile, whom I discovered chatting with the bus driver and other colleagues in a cosy office. They were all enjoying hot coffee. It was explained to him that unless he forthwith secured our entrance to his luxurious palace, he would be severely kicked in the ass all the way back from Versailles to Paris. Reluctantly, he began to stir himself.

Eventually, after a long, tedious dispute concerning tickets, in a dripping huddle, grumbling and muttering, we forced our way into the over-decorated State rooms, whose high ceilings were bright with allegorical paintings, framed in bronze. On surrounding walls hung brilliantly coloured Gobelins tapestries, portraying ladies of the Court as semi-clothed nymphs and shepherdesses. Marble statues lurked in hidden niches. Everywhere, Kings of France defeated their enemies, securing Glory and Repute throughout the Civilised World. Our multi-lingual guide now wound himself up and went into overdrive.

'This' (he told us) 'was an original model for all the grand palaces of Europe: Bourbon and Hapsburg. Until 5th October 1789, it had been a complete world of luxury and splendour. Ten years later, it was a desolate shell, destined to become the museum of museums, where generations of gawping foreign tourists (like us) would come to apprehend the life of France's glorious past ... and be systematically moved on from room to room.

'*Avançons, messieurs, 'dames...*'

We advanced through the Hall of Guards into the Hall of Mirrors – very tarnished. Through the tall windows you could look into the park and see broad walks and ponds against a background of little copses and imitation classical temples. This scene was shrouded in rain and mist. The palace was very cold. We dried our streaming hair with dirty handkerchiefs. Those who had raincoats shook them surreptitiously in corners. In reply to repeated questioning, Monsieur Théophile told us that all lavatories in the Palace were that day closed for essential repairs.

He continued: 'In ze gardens, zey have fireworks. Zey have big fountains spurting up in ze sky. Zey have luvverly girls who dance ze ballet. Zey have places where zey all refresh zemselves.'

'That's what's we need,' everyone chorussed.

'*Avançons, messieurs, 'dames...*'

We advanced into the next room.

'Here ze bedroom of Marie Antoinette, ze queen. Here, she have her babies, which is big spectacle for her friends. Everyone come and watch. They say to her: "Open wide, please!" So she open legs very wide. Out come babies. Ze bedroom very crowded. Very interesting to have new prince. Get very 'ot. Louis sixteen, he open zis window to get some fresh air.'

Théophile tugged at the window to demonstrate Louis' famous gesture. The story was that when Marie-Antoinette was giving birth to her first child the room got so hot and crowded she almost suffocated. Then Louis opened the window and succeeded in reviving her with a blast of cold air. When Théophile opened it a shower of rain hit him in the face and he struggled to close it, wrestling helplessly with the catch. This was better. We began to snigger. Life was returning to its normal state of comic absurdity.

'*Avançons, messieurs, 'dames...*'

In the next room, Théophile catalogued for us major events of Court life pre-1789: 'Three kings live here: fourteen, fifteen, sixteen. Fourteen and fifteen fight many battles and win them all. Sixteen not so wish to fight as he like to stay ere in Palace. E ave problems. E orphan when young. E grow up, e meet luverly queen, e marry er, but e no ave baby. She no ave baby. E ave big problem with his foreskin. Then seven years after e marry er, e ave operation. Then e is OK, and e start aving children. Marie Antoinette, she is cross at long wait, she want all night to ave pleasure.'

This was well received. It was the best story of the day and people began to wriggle with suppressed laughter and embarassment. Girls nudged each other.

'*Avançons, messieurs, 'dames...*'

We advanced into the next room.

'All ze life of zis Court go on in public. All ze people come in to see ze king eat is dinner. Zey sit at tables in zis room. Kitchens is four hundred metters away, so food is brought by many, many waiters. It get very cold. All people watch as food pass. Gentlemen take off ats and bow. Ladies courtesy.'

Into the next room.

'Here is ze bedroom of ze king. He get up from bed. Ze noblemen come and elp im. Zey give im is closes. Zey powder is vig. It is called ze "*Levée*"...'

'The what?'

'Ze get-up. All ze people come to ask favours, make complaints, meet friends, have breakfast...'

By now his audience was thoroughly engaged.

'Zen ze king, e sit on the *chaise percé*, just ere. Is nice chair wiz ole in seat, so e can do *la grosse commission*. You know what is *la grosse commission*? E do caca on zis chair, ere, while zey all stand and talk wiz im.'

'During his breakfast?'

'Sure. E do it during breakfast and after breakfast...'

But his audience was no longer listening. The vision of Louis at his historic matutinals was overwhelming. We doubled up in helpless laughter. The oldest lady in the party, known to her chums as 'Gran', lay down on the priceless Aubusson carpets, helplessly kicking her legs in the air. Another lady burst into tears, revealing the pent up emotion of the morning. The girls clung together sobbing hysterically. It was a classical *fou rire*, lasting at least ten minutes. Other groups of tourists coming into the room were infected by it. A wave of laughter swept over them, without their knowing what had been the joke. Even the uniformed attendants were laughing at the laughter. The secret passage along which the queen had fled from the mob echoed with it. The only person not laughing was poor Monsieur Théophile who said to me in French, 'I do not understand what is the big joke. Have I said something wrong?'

'No, nothing.'

'Then why are you all laughing at me? I think your friends are very insulting to laugh at my English. Anyway, English is my third language. Normally I do this work with German tourists, but my colleague was absent today, and so I was allocated your English party. Unfortunately, I haven't been speaking English for some time, and I've lost all my fluency.'

'It's nothing to do with your English.'

'They are all laughing at me simply because I can't make the true sounds in your language. That is very cruel and very bad manners. They can't make the correct sounds in French, but I would not laugh at them.'

'Your English is fine. They are laughing at your description of Louis doing "*la grosse commission*".'

'I see nothing humorous in that. Now you are making excuses for them because they are your compatriots and you are ashamed of them. So you should be. They are anti-French and they are laughing at our past history – the story of our nation, which we in France respect and treasure. That is despicable conduct.'

'No, no, I assure you, not at all.'

But Théophile remained inconsolable. His stream of information dried up completely and his sulk lasted the rest of the day. Fortunately, by the time we'd completed our laborious pilgrimage through the State Rooms the rain had stopped. The skies cleared and a hot sun appeared. Steam rose from the sodden shrubbery in the park. The churches of Versailles were striking one, and it was time for our relaxing summer picnic. We found somewhere for lunch, a small free space, occupied neither by flower-beds, lakes, fountains nor marble statuary.

Gran cut the cheeses into chunks with my knife whilst I tore off lumps of baguette for us all, not forgetting Théophile. He accepted his share silently and with ill-grace. The rest of us from time to time punctuated our lunch with great cackles of obscene laughter. By now we'd forgotten our bad temper, the rain, and even what had made us laugh in the first place. It had become a good party.

Not until we climbed down from the coach at the Victoire, did Monsieur Théophile manage to recover some professional composure. He positioned himself very effectively by the exit door, to ensure individual 'au revoirs'. We all contributed generously, to compensate for our bad behaviour earlier, but he remained unmoved.

On final parting he shook me formally by the hand, saying, 'Au revoir, monsieur.'

'Au revoir, Monsieur Théophile, and thank you for all your help as our guide today. What you told us was most interesting.'

'Tourism is my profession, monsieur, but that is by necessity. It is not, you should understand, one that I particularly enjoy. One has, unfortunately, to meet some very disagreeable people. Like your compatriots. Extraordinary race, you English. As a historian, I can never forget that it was your nation that was responsible for the murder of Joan of Arc. That occurred in

1431, you know, much earlier than the events I have been recapitulating today.'

'Thank you for that additional piece of information.'

'Not at all.'

In the evening, whilst waiting for J-P to collect me for his promised dinner party, I recounted to Henri the exciting events of the day. He responded contemptuously.

'I have noticed, William, that the English find the acts of bodily excretion extremely amusing, but they are, as you know, perfectly natural phenomena.'

'It was the contrast between the formalities of the Court, and morning "*grosse commission*" that we found funny.'

'Why was that funny?'

'Because it was so lacking in dignity.'

'Actually, I have read that that account of events is quite untrue.'

'Really?'

'Yes, the version that he always performed "*la grosse commission*" whilst eating his breakfast was put about by revolutionaries, to discredit the monarchy.'

Further historical revelations had to be postponed because at that moment J-P arrived, greeted us and looked me up and down:

'Is my appearance satisfactory?'

'It would be better if you looked more English. You are too dark. They will not believe you are Anglo-Saxon.'

'I'm sorry.'

'It's not your fault.'

We set off wildly through the streets and squares of Paris in a borrowed Renault *deux chevaux*, J-P determinedly displaying his driving skills and knowledge of the city. We headed along the Champs Elysées towards the sixteenth district, where dwelt the rich and smart, behind high walls and even hedges! J-P turned towards me to explain.

'Later in life, William, I shall probably live in this *quartier*, which is appropriate for a doctor with a lucrative medical practice. One will easily visit one's rich patients.'

Being preoccupied with his future distracted him from the present and he failed to observe a large lorry and trailer crossing our eccentric path. We hit the trailer side on and came to a swerving halt.

'*Merde, alors!*'

Everyone descended into the street to survey the damage, apparently slight, and to apportion blame – not so slight – whilst I nursed my elbow, severely banged on the door handle. When J-P got back in and reversed to disengage himself, it appeared his nose was bleeding, but whether from contact with the dashboard or with an angry fist was uncertain. Otherwise, we had survived without damage and the car seemed to go more smoothly than before. It had been built to accept such set-backs, and so, in his way, had J-P. But his flow of speculation concerning his prosperous career had been cut short, and to that extent he was subdued.

On arrival, it was made clear we were late. The Dubois family were assembled in their green and gold salon to meet us and succeeded in conveying they had been there for some time. We all shook hands with each and told each other that we were delighted to make one another's acquaintance. This took further time.

There was no question of any aperitif, but on the way into dinner J-P tripped on a rug and fell awkwardly, hitting his leg against a small table. The Dubois family examined the table carefully for bruising. This second mishap confirmed the evening was destined to be a social disaster.

The family spoke urgently amongst themselves.

'That is the table which was bequeathed to us by your father.'

'Yes, it is quite valuable.'

'Your father believed it to be a good specimen of Louis Seize.'

'He was right.'

'He had an excellent knowledge of the furniture of that period.'

Madame Dubois was fat, and cheerful at the outset. But the

three girls made it clear they'd been assembled under protest. Monsieur Dubois, who spoke very precisely, was a senior doctor at the teaching hospital where J-P was an interne. During the entrée he launched a preliminary and devastating salvo.

'I have to tell you, mon cher Jean-Pierre, that the tutorial committee was deeply dissatisfied with your progress this year. I am telling you this informally, of course. You have not been zealous in our attendances and your punctuality has been questioned. Your capacities in dissection have not been fully demonstrated. There is a certain natural clumsiness, an example of which one has just witnessed.'

J-P's response to this attack was silent sulk, leaving me to go it, conversationally, alone. Unnerved, my command of French began to falter. My bruised arm was painful, I thought my trousers had been torn, and there were too many forks. Failure to use the subjunctive mood, after '*Il est préférable que...*' provoked a delighted chorus of correction from the three blonde, elegant and indistinguishable girls. Recognising there would be opportunities to patronise and correct, they cheered up enormously.

The eldest said: 'The French language is difficult for you, *n'est ce pas*? That is because it is such a sophisticated language.'

'How do you find English?'

'We are not interested in English. No one in Paris wishes to learn English since the betrayal of France by the British in 1940...'

'In any event, we are all committed to learning scientific subjects...'

'So that we can follow in the footsteps of our father...'

'Who comes from a family of doctors.'

'I see.'

The salad for openers had been dull but acceptable. The guinea fowls now served were wizened, dry and inedible. They had perhaps suffered from our late arrival, or had died from old age and starvation. All our skills in dissection were severely tested, and it was gratifying to observe that even Monsieur le docteur got into difficulties. Whilst working away, we took gulps of Pomerol red, which was manifestly sour and corked. Madame's cheerfulness faded, and silence began to descend on the dinner party. In an effort to play host Monsieur expounded to me the political realities in France. The whole government was undoubtedly corrupt and took bribes to maintain their mistresses.

'We deeply resent the coca-colonisation of France,' he went on. 'You Americans think you can buy up the whole country for a few dollars.'

'I am from England.'

'Much the same thing. Anglo-saxons have the same attitudes, whichever side of the Atlantic they live on.'

During the cheese, which was powerful – goat, or possibly tiger – even he began to weaken. The girls openly consulted their gold watches, indicating they had completed their tour of duty and expected to be stood down. At the coffee stage they were released. Their departure had none of the formality that had marked our arrival. They nodded and vanished, heavy with contempt. J-P who had been restless, excused himself, and a leaden silence descended, broken only by the sound of the lavatory flush. He returned looking more comfortable.

When at last, we'd expressed thousands of thanks and escaped, he said, 'Soon, I shall escape from my life as an impoverished and humble student and join that smart world.'

'That will be nice.'

My feeble reply provoked him.

'Well, my friend, what did you think of our evening?'

As he had taken the trouble to engineer the invitation I could hardly tell him exactly what I thought. After all, I was a foreign guest.

'Interesting.'

Driving smartly through a red light, J-P told me: 'You will undoubtedly receive a second invitation. That will give you an opportunity to establish yourself with one of the girls. Which one did you prefer?'

112

'I was unable to form a judgement.'

'William, you must be more positive if we are to progress your sentimental education. You will find that Ann-Sophie, the eldest, is the most sophisticated, but the middle sister, Lorette, is probably kinder. They are all very good in bed.'

'You're boasting.'

'Not at all. They all admire me very much.'

Our wild journey home was inducing terrible nausea, but I said politely, 'I thought Madame was most hospitable.'

'Yes, she too is good in bed.'

With difficulty, I opened the window and vomited guinea fowl and Pomerol into the rue Faubourg St Honoré.

On the afternoon of the next day, when we were again sitting in the salon, Henri asked, 'Have you read any of the works of Charles Fournier?'

'No, never.'

'Paris, you will understand, William, is a city of love, lust and passion, which prides itself on its capacity for logic and reasoning power.'

'I thought you regarded it as the City of Light.'

Henri was contemptuous of my English quibble.

'The point, my dear William, is that when all these conflicting elements come together the result is often absurd. For example, in the eighteenth century, a Utopian philosopher called Charles Fourier set himself the task of clarifying the passions. He came up with thirteen different varieties: the five senses, plus honour, friendship, love and parenthood, concordance, intrigue, and finally unityism.'

'What on earth is that?'

'It is a sort of egotism turned inside out.'

'Ah.'

'He believed that in a perfect France all these passions would be duly satisfied. The very planets, he was convinced, regularly copulated amongst themselves, so spawning civilisation as we know it.'

'Really! I would never have believed it!'

'Yes, and according to Fourier, no woman would have less than four husbands or lovers simultaneously.'

'What about men?'

'The "butterfly passion" for variety would apply.'

'What does that mean?'

'Magic reposes in the number thirty-seven. There would be thirty-seven million poets in the world. Thirty-seven great dramatists....'

'And we'd all be allocated thirty-seven girls each?'

'Fourier does not say that, William, but I do concede it is an interesting possibility.'

As to how these delightful fantasies were to be achieved? Henri – and presumably Fourier – was naturally precise.

'In 1838, Fourier established the first of a number of communities, where a hundred members of both sexes lived in physical and moral harmony.'

'Rather like the Victoire.'

My flippancy was poorly received.

'Not at all. You see, there was free love.'

This was the ingredient which had set Henri's imagination stirring. He was to be seen surreptitiously reading Fourier's *Theory of Four Movements* under his hotel desk. From time to time he smiled to himself as he contemplated images of this visionary world.

The Revd Mann was still to be seen, but evasive action had become a daily routine.

On passing in the evening at aperitif time, I spotted him slumped low in a seat in Bar Victoire. As his holiday was almost at an end, I stopped for a quick word on my way back to the hotel.

'Have you had a good day? Mr Mann?'

'Every day I've been visiting the same old haunt ... yes, good, I think.'

'Whereabouts have you been?'

'Ménilmontant.'

The Reverend seemed more direct in his replies this evening. Less pompous and smug. On the table before him was an almost empty bottle of Pouilly Fuissé, a luxurious wine by prevailing standards. At last, he was beginning to enjoy the delights of Paris, instead of worrying about his beastly flock of sheep, human and animal. It gets to them all in the end, I thought.

'What took you there?'

'It was where I went on my first visit to Paris, when I was engaged to be married to Clara. I went to Père Lachaise,' he said, staring at me unseeingly, his mind reliving the events of 1920.

'I saw the tombs of Molière and La Fontaine. And Héloise and Abelard. I thought about them. Abelard was a scholar and a priest like me. He loved her, you know. I thought about all the experiences that they had had. The rich lives that they'd led. The blessing of love. I decided it was time for me to live a little. And to love... All I'd done with my life had been to read great books about other people's experiences. Then I went to Ménilmontant and sat in a café for a glass of wine.'

'Just as we are now.'

'Yes ... No ... it was all different then. It was nearly thirty years ago, you see. Yes, I was your age then. I wanted to experience all of Paris, everything, wine, women...'

'Song?'

The facetiousness went right past him.

'Music, yes, everything. Particularly girls. I wanted a girl, you see, because I'd never had one.'

It was time for another drink, but it would have been absurd to have broken across the rich flow of memory.

'What happened?'

'They told me that Ménilmontant was a good place to go. To meet a lovely girl. You see, I didn't know what to do. How to pick her up, or what you did afterwards.' He poured the remains of his bottle into his own glass.

'Did you manage all right?'

'What? Manage? Yes, I managed very well indeed. Very well indeed. She was lovely, you see. It was a wonderful experience. She was very dark and petite, with beautiful breasts and thighs, and she took me back to her little room and showed me how to make love, and she was very kind and patient with me. I stayed with her for a long time. She showed me different positions. She knelt on the bed, and I came into her from behind. Yes, I remember that I particularly liked that one. After a short sleep, I wanted to do it all over again, but she said I had to go because her child was coming home. So I gave her some money and went, but I could hardly walk because I was so amazed by it all...'

'Did you arrange to meet her again?'

'No, no, no I couldn't do that.'

'Why not?'

'Because I'd sinned terribly, and I couldn't sin again. Don't think I wasn't tempted. And I've been fighting temptation ever since. Yes, even today. I've had terrible thoughts, terrible... You see to commit fornication like that was an unforgivable sin, one that has stayed with me throughout the whole of my life. I had betrayed Clara.'

'You weren't yet married to her.'

'I've thought about that girl every night for thirty years, relishing the wonderful experience I had. That hour has always stayed with me. Beautiful, moving. And, at the same time, I have been continuously mortified at my sin.'

'It was only once.'

'Even on the first night of my married life I thought about her ... about holding her ... seeing her beautiful body, smooth and white.'

'Let's buy another bottle of wine.'

He handed me the francs without even looking at me, and I caught the eye of the patron, who had been anxiously awaiting this moment.

Without any prompting, the Revd John began again.

'I haven't been able to come to terms with my past, you see. The terrible experience of adultery in Paris has been like the devil on my back for thirty years, but finally I decided to confront Him – yes, Satan in his lair – and come again. So I have come to defeat the enemy and recover my lost Faith.'

'And have you succeeded?'

'I have been back to Ménilmontant. To sit all day in the café where I met her.'

I thought of the Charles Trenet 1939 song, still very frequently played:

Je suis pas poète mais je suis ému,
Et dans ma tête y a des souvenirs jamais perdus...
Ménilmontant ... C'est là que j'ai laissé mon coeur...

'Did you meet her again – or her ghost?'

'No. I've sat each day in the café, watching the girls come in. She would be my age by now, about sixty? but I can't help thinking of her as she was.'

'Did you recognise anyone?'

It was a fatuous question.

'That was what I came to Paris for. To confront the past.'

'You might have been tempted to sin again.'

'That was the terrible, sickening thing. I wanted another girl. Or the same one. Any girl. I was desperate for one.'

Before he could say any more, Monsieur Henri, who had been standing at the bar, walked over to us saying in French, 'What an agreeable surprise to see two Englishman enjoying a glass of French wine. I hope you have been spending a pleasant evening together.'

'*Nous parlons du passé, des années après la guerre, des souvenirs jamais perdus.* We've been talking about the past, about youthful memories.'

'*Vraiment?*'

The Revd John ignored Henri's interruption.

'You see,' he said to me, in a voice broken by self pity, 'when I came on this trip to Paris it was because I have been experiencing a crisis in my life – a crisis of Faith. He led me into temptation then, and He as been leading me into worse temptation ever since. During all the forty years since I was here I have continued to torment myself. Women have long since ceased to have meaning for me, and I have never made love to any woman since having fornicated with that one beautiful creature in Paris. Not even my own dear wife. Instead, I have been drawn relentlessly to our own sex. You, Mr Soames – may I call you William – you yourself have attracted me since we first met.' He put his hand a little shakily on my shoulder. 'This is the terrible, irresistible impulse which, over many years, has destroyed my Faith.'

'*Comment?*'

Henri was anxious to understand all this, and I struggled to give him a simplified translation.

'*Monsieur explique qu'il avait une crise de foi.*'

This really confused him.

'*Une crise de foie? Une crise de foie! Ça c'est très sérieux. Vous savez que le foie est un organe très délicat, annexe au tube digestif, qui sécrète la bile, et qui remplit de multiples fonctions. C'est certainement à cause du vin blanc que vous buvez.*'

Henri pointed contemptuously at the bottle of white wine.

'*Je vais lui proposer un petit remède qui est toujours très efficace, mais je vous conseille de boire toujours du vin rouge...*'

'What's he saying?'

That was another translation which it was better not to attempt.

'He says he hopes you resolve all your health problems, and he invites us to join him in a glass of red wine as a remedy.'

'Alas,' Henri told me later, shaking his head, 'Fourier himself would have had real difficulty in allocating the Revd Mann's passion amongst his thirteen different varieties. But then, he wasn't French, so Fourier would never have made the attempt.'

When he and his party left next morning, the Revd John Mann avoided meeting my eye.

During this week Henri's relationship with Mrs Polianski continued to develop – but slowly, as might have been expected. They had little time for contact, and they needed to cross a fearful communication barrier. That it progressed at all demonstrated that language is an optional extra for the human species, that it is practicable to find love without speech. This was particularly true in France, where eye signals, arm gestures, and body movements can be an effective substitute. Henry used gestures designed to signal onset of disaster, incredulity, incomprehension and contempt. Mrs Polianski could match him in all respects, and watching them together was like watching a performance of ballet. Both moved bodies unselfconsciously, in a way the English find embarrassing.

During their allotted week at the Victoire, the shopping expeditions of mother and daughter mounted to fortissimo levels, impressing us all with the power of the dollar against the French franc, and confirming us Europeans in the view that the streets of New York were littered with the stuff. At the end of their week, they were to set off to what Anglo-Saxons called the 'Riviera', although in French this meant Italy: the Gulf of Genoa. This semantic difference required half an hour of interpretation time, most of it spent in convincing the parties, who were inclined to take independent views of the issue.

On their last morning a taxi was summoned to take the Polianskis to the Gare de Lyon, and a crowd of friends and admirers gathered in the hall for the excitement of a departure. There was confusion about luggage, and an arriving guest had to recall his suitcase which had been loaded into the Polianskis' cab. Mrs P gave us both a smacking, but impersonal, kiss and squeezed into the back seat amongst bags and boxes old and new. We were retaining more baggage in the *consigne* of the hotel, pending their return, as they would spend the final night of their Grand European Tour at the Victoire before sailing away to 'little ole New York' in the *Normandie* from Cherbourg. This, also, was impressive stuff.

119

'Oh Revour, youse guys,' they shouted through the cab window, and the old Citroen got up off its knees and rattled off, leaving us with the sensation that brightness and life had gone from the hotel.

Henri said, 'One must admit she has a powerful personality. She is very vivacious. Not like an American. One might even think she was French...'

This was a high form of praise.

'Perhaps from Touraine or Limousin. Not further south than that.'

'I should guess her family came from Poland originally. They must have gone to the United States amongst the huddled masses.'

This theory delighted Henri.

'So she is really from Europe?'

'Aren't they all?'

'The Americans?'

'Of course.'

'Ah!'

The fact that Mrs P was in reality a European seemed to alter Henri's perception of her. When she had been an American she had been a tourist, member of a remote species, to be humoured and supplied with professional services. As a 'European', she could properly be regarded as an individual in her own right.

'When they come back,' he said thoughtfully, 'perhaps we will invite them out for the evening. Do you think we could do that?'

'They'd love it.'

'What do you think of her, William?'

'She's very American. What do you think?'

'She is fat and desirable.'

'Undoubtedly.'

'We will have dinner at a brasserie.' This was Henri's idea of a fashionable night spot, formed some years earlier. 'We will eat lobster and drink *vin d'alsace* ... we will have a little party ... I shall invite the Polianskis and you, William and perhaps Jean-

120

Pierre, for he speaks excellent English and they will find him amusing.'

'And he can look after Trudy.'

This was Mademoiselle Polianski, who appeared silent and unmoved during all her mother's emotional outbursts. Thin and blonde, but not unattractive, it was impossible to know what she was thinking, or, indeed, whether she was thinking at all.

'And for you, William,' he added, 'we must find a young and beautiful French girl. An educated creature, on whom you can practise your command of the French language, and who has the capacity to correct your errors of grammar and style.'

Mention of a 'jeune française' was sufficient to call to mind the lovely Jacqueline, who'd walked in beauty as the night of cloudless climes and starry skies.

Henri was saying, 'Admit that American women do not attract you. They encourage your English snobbery. Admit that you dislike them because they are rich, superficial, and have bad manners. Is that not so?'

Would I ever find her again? Henri was waiting for a reply to his question.

'I had supposed that those were your views, Henri.'

'You were right,' he said gravely. 'I had thought that. Generally, in the past, I have found the American race to be not yet civilised. But Madame is exceptional. She is a racial phenomenon, don't you agree?'

'Undoubtedly.'

I concluded that Henri's relationships with the opposite sex were hopelessly polarised: a curious compound of the strictly commercial and the naively romantic. The commercial could be sub-categorised as 'buying' – from Ann-Marie – and 'selling' to the widow with the spaniel. The romantic seemed to be focused on the Victoire itself, the one continuing love of his life, with whom he'd long lived in a state of quarrelsome matrimony. The romantic element in his character, on the other hand, had the potential to be transferred to almost anyone or anything. But then he was like that. Part of him was scientific and pragmatic, another part imaginative and insecure. I also decided that I was beginning to reason like Fourier...

Interlude

Ida wasn't prepared for the train journey from Paris to Juan les Pins, which lasted fifteen hours. It seemed longer. She'd once taken the Transcontinental from Chicago to New York, but had spent her first two hours being pursued by a Marine colonel in a buffet car. And the remainder in his private compartment. He'd been a very imaginative guy. Thus, time had passed quickly. On this trip, without any such distractions, she was seized with restlessness and impatience.

'Honey, I get so bored with foreign travel, I could cry,' she told her daughter several times during the evening.

'Why don't we just go home? This European crap is driving me nuts.'

A young steward came in to convert their cabin table into bunk beds, and she tried to engage him in conversation. He shrugged, nodded politely, and left without even soliciting a tip.

Climbing into her lower bunk, she said, 'You can't tell where you are with these French guys. Sometimes, I love them all. Other times, they make you feel like shit on toast.'

'Mom, I don't think you should say things like that.'

'Well, it's true.'

'So what?'

'So what did you think of that young English guy at the hotel?'

'Kinda cute.'

'Yeah.'

'Sort of intellectual, I guess. You know. Brainy.'

'So why didn't you talk to him a little? Warm him up for me?'

'I guess he wasn't interested in American girls.'

'Or even French girls.'

'Nope.'

'Those Britishers are all pansies.'

'How d'you know that, Mom?'

'You could tell from the way he spoke English. "Old boy", "Pip pip" and all that. Queer as a three dollar bill.'

'Why they all like that?'

'It's the goddam awful food they eat.'

'You're crazy, Mom.'

'And the climate.'

'Gee, Mom, I didn't think that guy was a pansy.'

'Why not for heaven's sake?'

'Well, I caught him trying to look up your skirt.'

'Shit, honey, everyone does that.'

'You're crazy, Mom.'

'These bunks aren't big enough for my ass.'

During the night, the train stopped and started several times, waking Ida from an uncomfortable doze. The cabin got very hot. She heard her daughter sleeping peacefully, and only just resisted the temptation to wake her up and renew conversation.

In the early hours of the morning, she said, 'Trudy.'

'Huh?'

'Wake up.'

'Why?'

'Cos I wanna talk to you about Paris.'

'What about Paris?'

'Didja think it was great? All that singing and dancing, and cheap fashions in shops, and cultural stuff?'

'Yeah.'

'D'you think I'm goin to meet a new fella on the Riviera?'

'Sure.'

'A regular French guy ... with a moustache ... a great lover.'

'Sure thing.'

'That hotel guy, Henri. Nothing pansy about him.'

'Howju know that?'

'I always know. He's a guy who gets it regular like cornflakes.'

'He was reely polite.'

'He was ready for it.'

'But howju know, Mom, about his getting it regular?'

'Well, he just looked at me, and I knew he was getting me undressed.'

'You always say that.'

'Well, it's true.'

'Sure thing.'

'It's all kinda difficult when you don't understand what they're talking about.'

'Sure thing.'

'Can't you say anything other than "Sure thing"?'

'Yeah.'

They struggled down their corridor for *petit déjeuner*, but couldn't drink any coffee. It was black and treacly, having brewed all night. The waiters spoke no known language. Orange juice, toast, doughnuts and pancakes all appeared to be unavailable.

'Europe is crap,' Ida said.

One of her moods was about to take over. Trudy knew the signs.

'Look out of the window, Mom. There's the sea. It looks reely great.'

The train was now making its way slowly along the littoral.

'What sea?'

'Mediterranean, I guess.'

'Well, shit in it.'

'Mom, you mustn't say things like that.'

They looked at the glittering waves, and Ida, try as she might, found it impossible to be angry for long. They dozed for a while. In another hour, their train stopped and deposited them with a mound of baggage on an empty platform at Juan. After it had pulled out there was silence, save for the seagulls. They badly needed a drink of iced water. The sky was unbroken blue and

125

the sun fierce. Although only eleven in the morning, it was already very hot, and both Polianskis were burdened with coats and hats. They sat perspiring on their baggage, dazed by light and heat, awaiting arrival of a Cook's tour representative. Time passed. Towards midday, they realised they were being assailed by mosquitoes.

Ida said, 'We should have brought that British tourist guy with us.'

'The one you thought was a pansy.'

'Pansy or not, he'd get us to a hotel.'

According to their tour papers they were to be lodged at Hôtel Quatre Saisons, and by showing this document to an ancient ticket collector, and waiting while he fetched his spectacles, they succeeded in securing an equally ancient taxi. There was some dispute as to whether it would carry all their luggage, but Ida prevailed.

They drove slowly down a country lane, bordered with pines, to what seemed a derelict farmhouse. Chickens scratched in a barren plot. There, they disembarked and were obliged to ring a bell for some time before a maid appeared. Then, having argued with management for a further period of time, they were, by early afternoon, installed in a relatively cool bedroom. They'd missed lunch. Heat and language barrier had reduced Ida to a state of irritable torpor. She fell into bed ignoring her mosquito nets, which proved a mistake. Trudy stared out of the window and wondered what Mom would be like when she woke. She might be thoroughly refreshed, ready for anything. That would imply 'going out and meeting the people'. And generally whooping it up. Satisfying her extraordinary appetite for life. Or, on the other hand, she might be aggressive, ready to pick a fight with the first person she met. And to complain about cleanliness of the bathroom. In that last respect she'd have plenty of scope. Or, worst of all, she might just sulk for the next thirty-six hours.

Trudy went outside and sat on the terrace in the shade, where a smiling waiter brought her a glass of *citron pressé*. He was tall for an Italian. His hair and manners were both highly polished. And his English was excellent.

'Where you come from in America, Miss?'

'Chicago.'

'I not been there, but I been to New York, Boston, Philadelphia. One year. Great country.'

'You said it.'

'I learn English. Get me good job here in France. Earn much money. Soon, I go back to USA.'

'Yeah?'

'You like it here. On coast, sun shine all day. You go on *plage* tomorrow? Swim?'

'Sure thing.'

'I go swimming in afternoons off work. Is good. I show you where to go. I meet you there.'

'Sure thing.'

'You like dancing?'

'Sure thing.'

'I take you dancing. I very good dancer.'

'Yeah?'

'In Casino. You like that. Many people. English, American, French. Nice music. What your name?'

'Trudy.'

'That nice name: Trudy. My name is Luigi Rocolo. I come from Genova. Big city. Like America.'

'Yeah?'

When Ida came in Trudy saw her face was covered in red swellings.

'Gee, Mom, you look terrible.'

'Well, shit to you, honey.'

'Sorry, Mom.'

'Thanks a bunch.'

Luigi reappeared at this moment and promised to supply cooling lotions from the private store which he kept specially for lovely American ladies in distress. He also counselled Ida to remain in her bed for the evening to recover from mosquitoes and heat. In the morning she would be a lovely lady again. He would be happy to accept responsibility for Trudy. He would explain to the management that Signora needed supper in her room. He would personally bring it to her. He would show her how to operate the mosquito net. In fact, he would take care of everything.

'Is no problem,' he repeated several times.

'That guy's an ass-crawling little creep,' Ida said ungratefully, but she retreated to bed, grumbling.

That left Trudy free to go off with Luigi after dinner to explore Juan. Luigi had abandoned his waiter's white jacket, put on a coloured shirt, and behaved impeccably. During the evening he told her the story of his trip to America in considerable detail, and outlined his life plan for the future. Several times. He would undoubtedly soon become rich and successful, and would own a restaurant and an Alfa Romeo motor car.

Trudy struggled hard to be impressed, but found it difficult.

'Tomorrow we go swimming on beach, yes?'

'Sure thing.'

Luigi had wanted to go dancing at the Casino, but Trudy pleaded fatigue after her journey. Luigi was sympathetic, and made no attempt to advance their relationship. He wasn't in a hurry. The Polianskis were to stay in the Pension for ten days. When Trudy got back to their bedroom Ida was awake – and spoiling for a row.

'How you been, Mom?'

'What do you care?'

'I had a great time, Mom.'

'Well, shit on you, honey.'

'Mom!'

'Well, whatdja wanna go off with that wop for? Leaving me ill in bed.'

'Mom!'

'We don't have to come to Europe for you to go off with little wops like that. Chicago's full of them.'

128

'He's a nice guy. Been to New York and all.'

'Should have stayed there.'

'Mom.'

The following afternoon was played out in the same way. Ida retired to bed, grumbling that her morning walk into Juan had been exhausting. Trudy met Luigi in the garden.

'You good swimmer, Trudy?'

'Nope.'

'I very good swimmer. Swim many kilometres across bay. Dive in from high rocks. Swim faster than my friend Antonio.'

'Gee whiz.'

Antonio had been cited before as substantially inferior to Luigi in various respects: particularly dancing, swimming, and making love. He was also a waiter – in a café in the town – and came from Genova. He might even be Luigi's cousin, or some other relative. Trudy was suddenly penetrated by an idea.

'Say, Luigi, why don't we get Antonio to come out with us one evening. Then we can ask Mom.'

At first Luigi looked doubtful, but he said, 'OK.'

'Will you ask him?'

'OK.'

When Trudy got back to her bedroom in the late afternoon her mother was simmering with suppressed rage. That others should be having a 'great time' whilst she languished alone in daytime heat was unfair. There were no other English speakers at the Pension, so she was totally isolated.

'We got a double date, Mom, I fixed it. You gotta guy called Antonio. He's a friend.'

'You're crazy.'

'He's a nice guy, Mom. Comes from Genoa. Like Luigi.'

'So what should I do?'

Trudy no longer felt guilty at deserting her mother. Generally, she didn't know which she most wanted: her mother's approbation, or to keep her pacified, or to make her happy. She knew her mother regarded the whole European trip as an opportunity to have a grand, irresponsible, romantic love affair – or several. So far there hadn't been candidates. Maybe this was it: Antonio was destined to become the one real souvenir Mom would take back with her. After all, that's what you come to Europe for, wasn't it?

When Antonio arrived it was apparent he was a poor replica of Luigi – short, and suffering from body odours. Mostly, he looked worried about something. Worst of all, he hadn't a word of English, so Luigi had to carry on conversation with both girls. He enjoyed that, but they didn't. After a few dances, changing partners, they all had drinks together on the terrace, for which Ida paid. It seemed to Trudy that the two Italians watched closely as Ida got notes from her purse.

A middle aged Frenchman asked Ida to dance, which cheered her up. Later, they walked back in separate pairs to the hotel where, as they parted, Luigi said, 'You very lovely girl Trudy. You gorgeous. I now love you very much.'

He gave her a powerful kiss, and put his hands on her breasts, to which she responded without enthusiasm. She was bored by Luigi, but then she always was by men. They talked about themselves for a couple of hours, and then wanted to rape her. Luigi was a typical specimen.

'You love me a lot, too?' he asked.

'Uh huh.'

She wrenched herself free.

In their bedroom, her mother said, 'That little guy smells.'

As it had been her scheme, Trudy felt called on to defend them.

'They're a couple of nice guys.'

'Shit, honey, I could do better than that in Pessary, Ohio.'

'This is Europe, Mom.'

'So what? Your guy's OK,' she said grudgingly.

'OK. We'll swap.'

'You will?'

'It's a deal.'

The next night, after they'd changed partners, it got better. They drank more cognac with water, and danced every dance. Antonio gave no trouble. Soon, Ida began to laugh a lot. Trudy had to stop her climbing onto a table and doing her war dance. At the end of the evening she and Luigi went off into the garden, and when she got into bed she was breathing heavily. Trudy, accustomed to such situations, pretended to be asleep. She'd disposed of Antonio by pushing him down the steps. He'd fallen quite heavily onto the concrete path.

On the last night of their stay, there was a 'surprise party' at the Casino, and they all set off together wearing fashionable clothes. The Italians were elegant in silk shirts and polished hair. Even Ida now conceded that Juan wasn't a bad little dump. It had been a late sunset, and now a gigantic moon was coming up over the sea.

'It's kinda romantic, Trudy.'

Luigi said, 'Is bad you go tomorrow. You stay, maybe, another week?'

Ida put her arms round him and gave him a big hug.

'Gee, honey, we would if we could.'

They rounded a corner, from which they marched together along the sea frontage. All the population was heading for the same destination. Coloured lights glittered in the trees. The atmosphere was still, warm and perfumed with azaleas. Ida was thinking that perhaps they would stay on another few days when she noticed a shabby woman in a head scarf standing outside the Casino. She was carrying one small child in her arms, with another holding her hand. She could have been a gypsy. Her complexion was very dark and her expression aggressive. It wasn't clear whether she was begging from patrons going in or waiting for someone.

Luigi stopped and said suddenly, 'I 'ave to go now.'

As he turned to run, the woman seized him by his arm, delivering a stream of angry Italian. Unable to understand a word of the language, Trudy nevertheless immediately grasped that

131

Signora Rocolo was less than pleased with her husband's behaviour. They disappeared into the distance, the woman screaming '*Bastardo merdoso!*', Luigi replying '*Vaffanculo!*' one child running behind. The other members of Luigi's party watched in silence.

Antonio looked around nervously. Then he shrugged his shoulders and made a gesture of helplessness. In a burst of linguistic proficiency, he said in English, 'Is not good.'

When they got back to Quatre Saisons, they had to do their packing. Ida was surprisingly philosophical about Luigi, commenting favourably on his physical capacities.

'That guy has got a reely big prick but, no sweat, Trudy, honey, there's plenty more where he came from.'

Trudy was impressed at her mother's capacity to rise above the situation.

'It was my fault, Mom. We shouldn't have swapped them over.'

'Dear Mister Soames, pass me the sugar please.'

'Here is the sugar.'

'Will you now pass the milk, please?'

'Here is the milk.'

'Do you prefer tea with lemon?'

'No thank you, I prefer tea with milk.'

Recognising that life at Hôtel Victoire provided a severely limited view of Paris society, I'd sought to push open other doors. Becoming an English language tutor might prove a more lucrative profession than tourism. An advertisement placed in *Figaro* had produced only one response on the telephone, a rendez-vous at 5.00 p.m. on the next Thursday was fixed at a smart address in Neuilly sur Seine.

My would-be pupil asked, 'Would a fee of three thousand francs an hour be appropriate?'

This amount seemed magnificent – a glass of *blanc ordinaire* at Bar Victoire cost only three francs fifty centimes! It would be possible to buy a new shirt...

'Certainly.'

'I would like our conversation to concern itself with cultural matters.'

'Certainly.'

'You will be punctilious in correcting my errors of phrasing?'

'Certainly.'

'Please come at 5.00 p.m. I think you will find the ambience at my apartment agreeably English.'

I was to tutor la Baronne herself at first; later, possibly Monsieur le Baron; then, doubtless, the children. During all this it was proposed we drink tea together, a pleasing English custom, and did one prefer Orange Pekoe or Typhoo tips? Clearly an entrée into what in France is called 'Ze heeg Leef.' This would demand smarter clothes and better manners.

The apartment was imposing. The baronial salon offered only low arm-chairs, requiring relaxed postures. This made it difficult to impose the idiosyncratic rules of English pronunciation and syntax. Fortunately, Madame la Baronne had no difficulty in expressing herself in English and, from the opening exchanges, it might have been difficult to determine who was tutoring whom.

Soon she plunged into unexpurgated autobiography.

'You will have read the famous history of Madame Bovary. Zat is the history of all women in France. We live in ze country and we see nobody. Nobody at all! We are alone all with ze servants. It is terrible.'

'*The* servants.'

'Yes, ze servants.'

'Not "ze" servants. "*The*" servants.'

'Yes, zat is right. My 'usband, he is away all day working at his bank. He is a very busy, very rich man, and he does not have time for his family. So I have to look after my daughters without his help. They are aged thirteen and fifteen years.'

'I would never have believed it.'

'You are a big flatterer, Mister Soames.'

Madame la Baronne was not young and beautiful but she had lots of bubbly charm, reminding me of Henri's warnings of a predictable nature. What he had said confirmed the preconception that Parisians occupied their nights – and days, for that matter – in illicit encounters. Husbands had little mistresses for whom they provided luxurious apartments. As in a Feydeau farce, he explained, spouses ran backwards and forwards across a well lit stage, trousers falling down, colliding with each other, confusing identities, ending the first Act hidden in closets. Sex was a riotous game which, in Act II, had them rolling across beds, ending in Act III with a comical reconciliation scene, after the deceived wife or cuckolded husband had secured a bittersweet revenge.

Was it different in real Parisian life? In detail, it seemed, but not in substance. Who would have thought that so elegant, refined and amiable a lady would have wanted to risk her reputation for half an hour of you-know-what on the settee? How did M. le Baron succeed in becoming a great financier, when so much of his twenty-four hours was allegedly taken up in the management of his multiple domestic life?

Undoubtedly, he was a powerful and dangerous fellow, a tall and commanding presence, who could seduce an actress and count his money at the same time. These reflections did not occur until after two or three weekly tutorials. By then all attempts at linguistic correction had been abandoned. Instead, the Baron's matrimonial shortcomings (and quite a length of inner thigh) had both been exposed. According to la Baronne, this passionate swordsman could no longer spare time for her.

'He has his mistress for many years. She is now aged fifty and a very uncultivated person. He has established her in rue de Provence, which is near the Galéries Lafayette, so that she can go daily and spend what she wishes on his account.'

'That sounds very cruel.'

'It is cruel, Mister Soames, and I have suffered much.'

'I find it difficult to believe.'

'However, it is, alas, all true.'

'How do you know all this?'

'I know about it because he tells me.'

'You talk about his double life?'

'He knows I am not jealous, not now. Ten years ago, I was jealous, but now I have accepted that he must do as he wishes.'

'That is very tolerant of you.'

'Yes, and it gives me a freedom I would not otherwise have.'

'That must be a compensation.'

'Ah, Mr Soames, you remember what Flaubert said about his heroine Emma?'

'No, I don't think so.'

'She rediscovered in adultery all the platitudes of marriage.'

This conversation became part of our established tea ritual. La Baronne would pour, discoursing in fluent English on her matrimonial situation, with particular reference to restrictions – and freedoms – accorded to her. She had sacrificed herself for her family. And what had been her reward? Precious little. It was

135

true she lived a comfortable life in an agreeable home with reliable servants and many friends. What she missed was the deeper relationship that every woman needs. That was the element for which she was still searching.

'And, Mister Soames, I have never – how you say? – utilised the freedom which I have been accorded. No, not yet.'

The correct answer to this confession eluded me.

'In the meantime, I have my family, and my books and my friends, and I am enjoying speaking to you in English again because it reminds me of my childhood, when I was at a finishing school in Ascot, Berkshire. Do you know Ascot? The English countryside is very agreeable in Spring and I used to go for long walks with my English friends, whose names I still remember. There was Elizabeth and Shirley and Pauline. Such English names. I often wonder what has become of them. I am sure they will all have married happily in the English fashion.'

'I don't think marriages are particularly happy in England.'

'Yes, they will have had faithful husbands and they will have been faithful wives, I am sure.'

As the tutorial hour drew to its close la Baronne usually sought sympathy.

'What do you think, Mister Soames, of my history? It is a sad story, is it not? Do you not think that I need comforting? By some sympathetic person, like you, who is kind and cultured, and to whom I can talk freely?'

I thought that the conversation was becoming dangerous. Not that la Baronne was unattractive, but it was critically important not to put in hazard the fee of 3000 francs a week, which had been transforming my Paris life. I had bought a new shirt, and put two into the laundry. Soon I would be able to afford shoe repairs. Nor was it absolutely clear that la Baronne was signalling invitations. Above all, there was the constant threat of the bold, bad Baron, who would, at the critical moment, come through the double doors of the salon – accompanied by a crash of thunder – catching me with my trousers down, metaphorically and literally.

On the other hand, perhaps 'English conversation' in the original advertisement had been a code-word for you-know-what. To resolve the problem I consulted Henri, knowing beforehand what would be his inevitable response.

'Mon cher William, the hour specified for your meeting with this lady was five to seven, and "*cinq à sept*" is in our language a locution implying joyful and illicit sexual activity. The reasoning is that during the hours between five and seven, one can hardly be expected to be still working, and it is far too early to be dining, so that no other activity can conceivably be envisaged for a truly French civilised person. On the way home, therefore, it is normal for one to stop off for a couple of hours, to fill in what might otherwise be a wasted part of the day.'

'Accepting your classical piece of Gallic logic, it will follow that the English tutor will soon, doubtless, be dismissed for failing to perform in accordance with valid custom and natural expectations?'

'William,' he said, 'you have correctly analysed the position. It is gratifying that you are now able to see things from such a French perspective.'

'You think I'm making progress.'

'Undoubtedly.'

'But I'm not sure I want to make love to her.'

'William, I'm disappointed. It is ungracious of you to decline to satisfy a lonely lady. It is also uncharitable, unmanly and unpatriotic. If you do not respond, you will certainly be dismissed and replaced.'

'Why is it unpatriotic?'

'Because you have told me she has a high opinion of Englishmen. You are disappointing her expectations and disgracing your nation.'

The terrifying prospect of being hung for treason concentrated the mind. Destiny had selected me to fuck for England, and that was a duty which no true Englishman abroad in the land of frogs dare fail to perform. At the next tutorial session the matter would, I decided, have to be put to the test. I began to practise the new vocabulary which would be required.

Now it was late August the end of the season was approaching and the profession of tourist guide was beginning to seem unrewarding. Too many lost brown suitcases. Too many late trains at Gare St Lazare. Too much Parisian 'everyone for himself', a legacy perhaps from years of enemy Occupation. Paris had become an inhospitable city, where life was harsh and brutal manners were formal and insular, foreigners regularly short-changed, strangers suspect, tempers on a knife edge. It was normal to be elbowed out of a bus queue, or pushed aside by policemen. The traditional view of England was of 'perfidious Albion' – betrayal of France at Dunkirk in 1940, failure to appreciate General de Gaulle, incapacity to understand the world of ideas. Food in England was understood to be so disgusting that no French person would ever wish to find himself there. How the natives themselves survived was a mystery. It had made Englishwomen infertile, and Englishmen into homosexuals.

At that time, in the late summer of 1949, France was still locked into a pre-war culture, on which the effect of existentialism had been negative: to discredit existing values without replacing them with anything positive. Individuals continued their lives of wartime Resistance, not against anyone in particular, but against everyone. All of us were trapped in Sartre's *huis clos*: a nowhere world. Civilisation was hollow and counterfeit, as André Gide had unhelpfully explained in his novel *Les Faux Monnayeurs*. Hell was simply other people.

By September Henri, his terrible old mother, British tourists, and Paris itself were beginning to close in and suffocate. How to escape? A beach, or a country town with a river bank, welcoming cafés, and lovely local girls? But what to do about money, now in short supply? Professionals could arrange their faces in a 'Don't-forget-the-guide' expression when saying farewell to clients. For amateurs, supplicant posture was difficult. Attempts to solicit gratuities had produced two Gauloises bleues and half a packet of Cadbury's chocolate bearing teeth marks – not much for twelve continuous weeks of courteous and patient assistance. The problem was solved by Frederico, now a senior and qualified (by experience) *professeur d'anglais*, who presented comprehensive courses on English language, society and culture at the Advanced Institute of Civilisation, located deep in the Loire valley.

'I am due one week's vacation, but I've got to find a locum,' he told me. 'You could do it for me. On a fee sharing basis, of course.'

'How did you get the job?'

'Charm!'

'What would it involve?'

'Living off the fat of the land in my room at the château. Local wine with meals twice a day. Unlimited. Lunch and dine with the director, an old army chap called Bagnolet, who's got an English wife, Lucy. And the students of course.'

'But the work?'

'Nothing to it. Conversation in English all day with frogesses from the very best families. It's a finishing school for girls – and you're not to touch them.'

'Why not?'

'It's in the contract: fucky-fucky is out.'

'That's OK for you.'

'Don't get personal, ducky. Anyway, they're not there for that. They all want to speak English, as part of the veneer of upper-class snobbery. In your free time, you socialise. Tennis, if you're strong enough, and walks in the woods talking about riding.'

'Riding?'

'They're all aristos. They only want to go to England to ride horses, get the feel of hot stallions between their thighs, and reward them with sugar lumps. The horses, not their thighs.'

'You make them sound a pretty unattractive bunch.'

'Well, hell, William, it's only a week.'

We haggled over the money. Cutting his percentage down to a reasonable proportion left a useful residue. What made the deal irresistible was that Madame did laundry for the staff. The prospect of lovely girls and clean shirts was very inviting.

When I arrived, after a dusty bus journey, the historic grey château was impressive – from the front anyway. The elegantly carved stone central staircase led to a locked door; there was no means of summoning attention. The servants' entrance was what I needed.

Wandering around to the rear revealed crumbling red brick and a notice indicating the historic building had been erected in 1911. It was a phoney château, fraudulent and pretentious, inhabited by phoney people. A back door opened at a push, revealing a dark, almost subterranean, corridor, smelling musty and rank with stale wine. Further along the corridor voices could be heard, raised and acrimonious. An ill-timed arrival, apparently… Standing indecisively in the dark, clutching my battered bag, it was impossible not to hear what was being said.

'You are spending too much money at the grocer's and too much at the butcher's. You have exceeded the systematic budgets which I set for you. Our business will not survive if you continue to spend at the current rate.'

'The girls have to eat, André. So do we. It can't be done for less. Your so-called budgets are not at all realistic for life in France today. You think you're still feeding your foreign legionnaires in Djibouti. As it is, there wasn't enough pot au feu to go round this evening. And wine is down to the last six bottles. These are young people from good families, and they are used to eating well.'

'I know, I know, but…'

'You must raise the fees.'

'There is no possibility of doing that, for reasons which I have many times expounded to you. It is already difficult to obtain additional…'

'We have no alternative if we want to keep going. We are coming to the end of the road, André. I cannot go on managing the place without money, and we are running out of it.'

This was the worst possible news. Paris suddenly began to seem attractive again. When was the next return bus? Probably tomorrow. For tonight there was no escape. Knocking loudly on the door and shouting 'Bonsoir!' evoked a suspicious response.

'Who are you and what do you want?'

'I'm William Soames. You are expecting me here to replace Fred Harvey. Enchanted to meet you.'

Neither the Captain, whose military moustache and hair were both greying, nor his wife could muster much warmth.

'Dr Harvey implied you were an older person...'

'With years of teaching experience.'

'I've been speaking English all my life.'

All this had been in French.

Now Lucy, who was small, fair and rather younger than her husband said in English, 'Where do you come from?'

'From London. And you?'

'Also from London. But we have to speak French, because André doesn't understand English.'

'But isn't he the director of studies at your English school?'

Lucy reverted to French.

'André is a world accredited expert in teaching techniques. He was the chief instructor of a Division of the French Foreign Legion, and he has taught French to soldiers of many different nationalities.'

'Really?'

'I will show you your room – or rather, Dr Harvey's room. We will meet at *petit déjeuner*, which is at eight. Your classes begin at eight forty-five. Would you like to follow me?'

As I'd not eaten since a frugal sandwich lunch, that was disappointing. And 'Dr' Harvey? That was rich. Was I to become 'Dr' Soames?

After so inauspicious a start, things could only get better. At breakfast, the croissants were freshly baked by Lucy and delicious. The coffee came in big bowls without handles. There was home-made cherry jam. Even the gallant capitaine was less surly, at least by comparison with his abruptness the previous night.

Lucy did the serving. Introductions took place. There was

141

Marguerite, Jacinthe and Hortensia, amongst other tender budding flowers. One rule of the college was that only English was to be spoken at meal-times. This created a formal atmosphere.

'May I please 'ave the butter?'

'Here is the butter.'

'Now may I please 'ave the jam?'

'I am passing you the jam.'

The classroom procedure was similar, but more lively. We sat in a cosy circle, five 'lovely' girls aged eighteen and nineteen and myself, debating in English the comparative delights of London and Paris, with particular reference to woollen goods in Selfridges and Harrods. Considerable expertise was demanded as regards quality, design and pricing. They were all extremely well dressed, glossy in 'English' twin-sets and plaid skirts, attentive but aloof. Their lives revolved around family homes in Paris, *maisons secondaires* in the country, horse-riding, racing at Longchamps, sailing at Deauville, tennis in the garden, evenings at 'cocktails' or the cinema. They knew that ideas hung in clouds over St Germain des Prés, but that was about all. No, at Café de Flore, you could get exceptionally delicious *coupes à la crème* with more strawberries than anywhere else. The people there were rather vulgar. What turned them on was the life of the British Royal Family. Princess Elizabeth had recently married Prince Philip of Greece in Westminster Abbey, and her dress and veil came in for informed criticism. Did I go shooting in Scotland? And hunting with The Quorn? Some evasiveness was needed to mask a lack of detailed experience of these key elements in English Life and Society. At least two of the girls were lovely, but remote. Mostly, their attitude towards their English tutor was of polite condescension. He was a hired help, whose only redeeming feature was that he shared nationality with the royalty, dukes, earls and barons of England. France might have been republican for a century and a half, but class remained a powerful force in French society.

On my last day, our 'discussion group' was joined in mid-afternoon by Lucy Bagnolet. '*La pauvre anglaise*', as they called her behind her back, seemed tired – not surprisingly because, as well as teaching, she ran the château, did all the cooking, and waited at table. The girls treated her like a servant, sometimes using '*tu*' when giving her orders.

When the class ended, she said, 'You're very good with them. Would you like to stay here? I'm sure André would give you a permanent job.'

'What about 'Doctor' Fred?'

'He's lazy, and a frightful pansy to boot.'

'Isn't that an advantage here, with so many nubile girls?'

'No, they can see he's not interested in them and it turns them off. They can see you are interested, and they respond.'

This was encouraging. Having tapped a rich vein of frankness, it became easier to ask personal questions.

'You work terribly hard. Don't you ever take a day off?'

In response, Lucy looked at me, as if for the first time.

'Sometimes I go to Paris for a few days, which is nice...'

'Paris is always nice,' I heard myself saying.

On the last evening of the week's 'course', there was to be an English 'cocktail' for staff and students. In the morning we all departed early. For this grand climax we were enjoined to dress formally (which presented problems), and prepare our English conversation. It was intimated that one word of French would justify the blackest of marks in reports sent to parents and guardians. During the afternoon the girls were paired off in corners, practising.

'How do you do?'

'It is kind of you to come.'

'I am very pleased to make your acquaintance.'

Their precise articulation won them congratulations, at which they simpered.

Towards cocktail hour, deemed to be six o'clock, it got very hot. All day the atmosphere in the salon had been heavy, and, in the distance, thunder could be heard. Despite the oppressive temperature – or perhaps because of it – the party was an unimaginable success from the first words spoken, which were:

'May I offer you a small drink?'

'That is most kind of you.'

'Not at all.'

'What a lovely party.'

'I am so glad you are enjoying it.'

The cocktails were ludicrously un-English – *kir royale* – cassis liqueur, topped up with chilled Epernay. They were not 'small', but huge, sparkling, delicious and magnificently, tremendously, overwhelmingly potent. In the gloomy countryside outside the château, lightning flashed and thunder crashed. Tiles fell from the roof, dogs barked madly, gutters overflowed. Windows banged, the ceiling dripped rain, but in the salon we didn't care. Gradually, the girls forgot all their English, started giggling, dancing round, pushing one another, and generally letting their hair down. There was nothing to eat because, apparently, in England eating was not the done thing. At gracious and elegant cocktail parties, mouths were not utilised for receiving food, but for witty and allusive conversation.

'Look at my knees, Monsieur William. Aren't they prettier than any English knees?'

'Much prettier.'

'And my thighs?'

'I need to see more of them.'

'Well, now what do you think?'

'Yes, very pretty, but could I see still more?'

In these early stages we exchanged profound ideas about philosophical matters, but soon we aristos got pie-eyed, which wasn't difficult to do. If there were any outside guests at the party they must have left early, because after a couple of hours of continuous drinking only a hard core survived: Lucy, the girls – some of them – and myself. The primmest had retreated, looking green; retching sounds could be heard in the distance, behind the thunder. The gallant and surly captain had also excused

144

himself. He needed to call on his banker, he told me – understandably, having regard to the cases of champagne consumed. That the school was a financial disaster seemed now explicable.

Undoubtedly, the stage was set for some outrageous occurrences. Such events often cast shadows before them. Perhaps it was the storm raging outside which had detached the cast from reality, moving it into a theatre of the absurd, beyond time and space. Together, we were playing out a one act farce, probably by Rabelais. I recollected the doctor's words on his death bed: 'Ring down the curtain, gentlemen: the farce is over.' But now, in the salon, it was ring up the curtain, the farce has begun. With a really attractive cast. These muddled reflections were interrupted by 'English folk-singing', which was part of the study course. It had become necessary to sit down for a few minutes, to re-establish bodily control. Meanwhile, Lucy was leading the girls in:

'She'll be coming round ze mountains, when she comes,
She'll be coming round ze mountains when she comes,
She'll be coming round ze mountains, coming round ze mountains
Coming round ze mountains when she comes...'

This was a great success. Lucy was flushed, smiling and transformed. She was wearing one of those little black cocktail dresses which every girl has in her wardrobe for just this occasion. With her long fair hair let down and a shoulder strap slipping, she looked younger than before. Much younger, and very seductive. She and the girls circled round the salon, chanting:

'She'll be wearing pink pyjamas, when she comes.
She'll be wearing pink pyjamas, when she comes...'

The young mesdemoiselles thought this hilarious, believing the song to be a hymn to English refinement, or perhaps they'd reached a stage when they ceased to care about good manners, and were revealing themselves as they really were coarse, vulgar and sexy, when smashed on champagne.

'And we're going to take zem off er when she comes,
And we're going to take zem off er when she comes,
And we're going to take zem off er, going to take zem
    off er,
Going to take zem off er when she comes.'

This brought the house down. Screaming with laughter, they gathered round *la pauvre anglaise*, and unzipped her little black dress at the back so that it fell to the floor, revealing black bra, panties and stockings.

'And we're going to take zem off er when she comes' they shouted, suiting their actions to the words. It would have been unfriendly not to join in the fun, and removing blazer and college tie seemed the least an Englishman could do in sporting participation and to demonstrate he wasn't in the least offended. The girls took this as a challenge, and crowded round shouting: 'And we're going to take zem off im when he comes.'

Allowing them to remove trousers wasn't difficult. Transformation from pretentious desmoiselles into hot blooded, lusty she-devils made it difficult to deny them anything. Whether it was the storm, or champagne, or proximity of so many girls, with and without clothes, it is impossible to say, but consciousness faded and a period of time passed uncertainly and kaleidoscopically. The only clear sensation was that France was a wonderful place and the French were marvellous people. I loved them all. So, naturally, I kissed them all. And they kissed me. When awareness returned, we were chasing one another up stairs, and along dark corridors. All the electric lights had failed. Finally, came recognition of falling into a bed – mine? Lucy and I both got in. A couple of girls, possibly Jacinthe and Hortensia, wanted to get in as well, but there wasn't room for all of us. They clambered around – making our bed into a flower bed, I decided – and gave us both cuddles and hot kisses.

They now demonstrated that they adored Lucy and were very kind to her in various intimate ways, perhaps to make up for their cruelty in the past. They were also kind to each other, and to me, and naturally I reciprocated. This happy exchange continued for some time, but it became more dangerous than the champagne, and I began to wish that they would all (but one) go away.

Ultimately, all of them (but one – Lucy) did go away, but in the course of a long and confused night one or two drifted back into bed. Possibly Marguerite, or even Jacinthe. It didn't matter very much. By now I was ready to welcome them back. During a brief sober moment, the morning after and return to Paris loomed as a terrifying prospect, to be banished by kisses or sleep. Outside, the rainstorm, tropical in intensity, continued unabated throughout the night. Once, all the château lights came on, to a chorus of girlish screams; then they quickly failed again, this time with a final bang.

It was mid-morning before I returned to reality, with aching head and dry throat. All my companions of the night had disappeared, and the château was silent. My clothes lay around on the floor. I put them on, clutched my pathetic bag and crept furtively out of the door through which I'd stumbled a week earlier. It had stopped raining, the air was fresh, sun rising, with promise of a fine, late summer day, one wholly appropriate for my mood of fulfilment and optimism.

'*Vive la France! Vivent les jolies françaises*... Marguerite, Claudine, Jacinthe ... *et, surtout, la jolie fille anglaise,* Lucy!' I shouted, running down the drive to look for the bus. I loved them all, even the pretentious ones, once they'd got *le feu aux fesses.*

When I got back to the Victoire, my optimism faded. Henri seemed downcast. He told me that he was again coming under heavy pressure from his mother to agree to the arranged marriage. It seemed she'd withdrawn her objections to the lady candidate – whatever they'd been – had done a new and improved financial deal with Maître Roustain, and would now even permit Henri to spend a little time with the bride-to-be. Henri, for his part, had attempted to argue his case on the basis of J-P's physiological assessment of the lady's child-bearing potential, but Maman had described this prognosis as childish nonsense. Neither Henri nor I were prepared to admit that this was so, but we recognised that it wasn't a convincing argument. My matching depression was because I'd forgotten to collect any pay for my week's work.

As consolation, however, Henri, in my absence, had made a teaching appointment with la Baronne for the next day, Thursday. The terrifying prospect, which he had held out – of being hanged for treason – now filled my mind. Yes, Destiny had indeed selected me to fuck for England, and that was a duty which no patriotic Englishman abroad in the land of frogs dare fail to perform. Now, my encounters with Jacinthe, Hortensia and all the other flowers filled me with new confidence.

Events moved as Henri had predicted. From the very start of the lesson, French conversation practice turned happily towards the theory of love-making, and the natural and sympathetic relationship which teacher and pupil had for each. It was duly followed by a more physical activity in which I acquitted myself – I thought – with sustained ability. After experimenting with a series of different positions, some calling for quite gymnastic skill, la Baronne, with skirt pulled up to her waist, rode me as if I'd been her favourite stallion, which I suppose I was. I bucked and heaved, snorted and drummed my hoofs.

Afterwards, la Baronne said, 'My dearest William, as I would have expected from an Englishman, you fuck extremely well. You have made me very happy. And you? Have I made you happy, my darling?'

(I noted her use of the conditional perfect tense in this context.)

'Yes, of course, my darling. But do you think the English are particularly good at fucking?'

'Yes, generally speaking. With the exception of those who are homosexualists, of course.'

'Well at least I'm not one of those buggers.'

'But, William, I never for a moment thought you were like that.'

'What was it you particularly liked about my fucking?'

'Let me see ... that it was slow – and how do you say? – rhythmic, like a Beethoven quartet.'

'I had hoped it was less serious, with more sparkle, comparable to Mozart or Haydn?'

'Perhaps you are right. I need to experience it regularly in order to form an accurate view. Now we must part, because it is nearly seven o'clock.'

On the next Thursday, having washed with special care, wearing my new shirt and repaired shoes, I sauntered in through the salon doors, smiling a quiet seducer's smile, to be greeted by a short, stout gentleman: the Baron himself.

'Madame is unfortunately absent today, so I am personally able to profit from your kind visit. Much needs to be done to perfect my English; in particular, my banking vocabulary needs attention.'

'I'm not very knowledgable about banking.'

'Nevertheless, from what Madame has told me, I'm confident you will be a great help.'

Once having suppressed guilt, and settled into the tea ritual, conversation went well. The Baron's English was less fluent than hers, and recourse to French was sometimes needed. Despite that, a cordial relationship was readily established. The Baron was friendly, unassuming and a good story-teller. Linguistic corrections he carefully noted. Soon he began to expound banking transactions in considerable detail with a wealth of French technical vocabulary. The mysteries of collateralised securities and revolving credits had to be first explained in French.

Translation was handicapped by an inadequate English vocabulary, but at the end of the hour, the Baron said, 'Monsieur Soames, you have been very patient, and I would like to have the benefit of your help again. But you will need to come to my bank at a time which is more convenient to me. At three p.m.'

He gave me a card, and we fixed a date. That made 6000 francs a week! That meant new shoes and a haircut.

When this development was reported to Henri, he became very negative.

'She is testing out your loyalty to her.'

'What loyalty?'

'As to whether you will keep faith.'

'Why would she do that?'

'Why? Because she wants to see whether your sentimental friendship with her will survive. If, however, you transfer your allegiance to the Baron, she will know that you are a betrayer of her trust.'

'You're putting it in very dramatic terms.'

'You must not go to him, or you will lose her.'

'I'm only giving them English lessons.'

'It is a trial of strength between them; as to which of them will win you over to their cause.'

'Can't I just give lessons to both of them?'

'That is not practicable.'

'It would be 6000 francs a week, and I could invite you to go with me to no. 122. It would be my round.'

This had seemed a compelling argument, but Henri was not persuaded. However, he reluctantly agreed to my giving one exploratory lesson to the Baron at his bank, probably because, like me, he was intensely curious as to what would happen.

Banque Geny, of which M. le Baron Geny was Président Directeur Générale, occupied elegant offices near the Bourse, a walking distance from the Victoire. That would make it convenient for a weekly lesson. Getting into the P.D.G.'s office, however, was like tackling an assault course. The first hurdle was a smart young usher in tail coat and grey silk cravat, who cross-examined me superciliously about the nature of my business. He passed responsibility to a uniformed messenger, who looked horrified at my lack of tie, jacket or creases in trousers. On the fifth floor a supplementary process of identification was needed to penetrate a private office. Here the path was barred by a delicious young secretary, who had been sitting in a ready-to-go posture in front of a typewriter without paper, looking slightly flustered. It was clear she had taken up her position when my entrance was announced – the top two buttons of her blouse were undone, and her elaborate hair-do needed attention.

'Monsieur Soames' she announced angrily, opening the door into the Baron's private quarters. The Baron was in an expansive mood, having, it seemed, recently returned from a late lunch.

'I am very fond of England and the English. The English are good judges of both horses and women. You have not, of course, visited my stables, but you have had the pleasure of meeting Madame la Baronne, and you have just encountered my little friend here.'

He nodded towards the outer office.

'What do you think, Monsieur Soames? As one man of the world to another, which will pass the finishing post first in your expert opinion?'

'They are both very charming ladies.'

'Yes, I adore them both.'

'Does not that present problems?'

'Not at all, Monsieur Soames. There are different kinds of love for different kinds of girls. For Madame la Baronne, I have uxorious love, because she has been a long-time spouse and companion. And the mother of my family. But sometimes a man needs more than that. He needs to express passion, spontaneous and uncontrolled.'

'He needs it for what reason?'

'For his health. A normal man needs passion, jealousy, excitement, danger which tunes him up each day for his work in his office. Without these stimulae he becomes bored with life, dull and liverish. Particularly in the afternoons.'

'Really?'

'Women,' said the Baron with absolute conviction, 'are the best natural medicine in the world.'

151

'So you need two of them?'

The Baron hesitated.

'Since we have been speaking with frankness and in confidence, between men of the world, I have to admit to you that there are three ladies in my life at present. Two of them, you have met: my spouse and my little friend. I also have a mistress. Once, she was *ma petite amie*, but that was some years ago, and her status has changed with the passage of time. She no longer excites passion, but I cannot desert her because she has been loyal to me. I have to concede to you, Monsieur Soames, that it is sometimes not easy having three demanding ladies in one's life, but there are compensations. It is, as you English would say, my only hobby – apart from my horses, of course.'

'Of course.'

'It is like a collection of foreign postage stamps. I have three excellent specimens and – who knows? – I may acquire more, or make an exchange.'

The Baron laughed aloud at this joke.

'Now,' he said, 'we must speak together in English about revolving credits.'

When I left the bank the cashier behind a glass screen gave me the 3000 francs in crisp new notes. But the Baron had not proposed another lesson. He had got much quieter towards the end of the hour. Back at the Victoire there was a telephone message for me from la Baronne. The course of English lessons was terminated for the time being. Not to call her: she would call me. Henri had been right. I had failed a critical test. But what exactly had it been?

Fortunately, I had little time to solve the problem, as other dramatic events crowded in. There came, in the middle of the next night, an anguished cry at my bedside.

'William, I have come to ask for your help.'

'What? What d'you want?'

'William, a tremendous event has occurred. Unbelievable! Incredible! Magnificent!

'What are you talking about?'

'William, my friend, I have at last fallen in love. For nearly forty years I have been waiting hopefully for this event and, enfin, it has come to me.'

'Congratulations and good night.'

'No, no, wake up, William, and listen.'

It was five o'clock in the morning; I'd fallen into bed only two hours earlier. More sleep was needed to extinguish memories of a desperate round of '*gaîeté* and *plaisir*': a long, hard night of eating, drinking, laughing, shouting, kissing, singing and dancing. My throat was dry, bowels churning, head aching, unprepared for an hour's French conversation practice. Without invitation, Henri sat down on my bed, beaming. He was apparently unscathed by the night's events, but needed to talk...

As the date of the Polianskis' return approached, he'd made no reference to the magnificent dinner party at Brasserie de Provence, to which he'd promised to invite them – and me. But his pattern of life was so established that minor changes were noticeable. He'd become more active and his homeopathic consultancies had substantially increased. More of his day was committed to being a doctor, and less to being an hotelier. The reception desk was often unmanned, and a tide of complaints mounted. Also, he ceased to visit no. 122 on Saturday nights! These variations from routine suggested that his former objects of desire – his beloved Victoire, and his Saturday night partner – had now been abandoned. Also, more pragmatically, that he was accumulating a secret reserve of funds needed to host a classical Parisian *nuit de gaîeté et plaisir* – a marathon 'night of pleasure', arranged to progress through traditional stages. First, there would be several rounds of aperitifs, probably Martinis or Pernod, whilst lovingly contemplating purple ink menus and conducting ritual discussion with the *patron*. All this was designed to create not so much a meal as a work of art, subtle and balanced.

Departure of the Polianskis for the Mediterranean a month

earlier had left us depressed, so their return should have been a joyous occasion.

However, checking in at reception, Ida announced, 'I'm smashed by all this travelling.'

Monsieur Henri, who had been practising various greetings from his English phrase book, replied, 'I tell you, Madame, is better to arrive than travel hopefully.'

'Say, Monsieur Henri, that's kinda worth thinking about.'

Whilst fumbling with their baggage, Henri whispered to me, 'Is she not truly statuesque? Resembling a painting by Boucher, or even Renoir, would you not say?'

'Certainly.'

The Polianskis had one last night in Paris, and next day were to take a train to Cherbourg, thence by luxury liner *Normandie* to New York. Their long summer European jaunt was at an end, for them, it was *fin de saison*. For us Yurropeans, there was another month to go.

Henri was right. Despite her fatigue, Ida looked very attractive, slimmer, and more tanned than when we'd last seen her. Trudy, as always, looked blank and bored. With Paris? Or with life in general? They obviously wanted to get to their room to recover from their journey, but Henri detained them with his courteous head inclination.

'It is my pleasure to invite you to dine with us this evening, your last night of vacation in Paris. We shall be having a little party in your honour. William will naturally be joining us, and my young friend Jean-Pierre, who is a doctor, and Ann-Sophie, his friend, who is very cultivated.'

'Hell, Monsieur Henri, that sounds twenty-three skidoo.' Both of us were baffled by this, but she added, 'Shall I wear my formals?'

We arranged to meet at nine o'clock, and retired to prepare ourselves for the long night of exhausting pleasure ahead. At first, conversation during dinner did not flow, because we were too early and the restaurant was silent and empty. Ida and a mute

Trudy were conscious of having over-dressed for the occasion, both in low cut, cleft revealing pink taffeta. Henri wore a striped brown suit with enormous shoulders and tight waist, which made him look like an apache in a silent twenties film. He was less comfortable off his home ground. The well-groomed waiters at the brasserie were unimpressed by my purple-dyed battledress trousers and shabby blazer.

There were language problems. J-P, who had arrived without Ann-Sophie, insisted on translating everything, which slowed down the flow.

The dinner took a long time. After the aperitifs, most of us chose an entrée of tender lobster mayonnaise, followed by chateaubriand steaks at least five centimentres thick, served '*seignant*' – which meant barely cooked at all. According to Henri these were to be regarded as *repas régales* – extra special treats – and were to be ingested at a stately pace, accompanied by polite conversation about the political situation, a flow of Pol Roger and carafes of vintage bordeaux rouge. After that, *salade* and a grand choice of *fromage*, then *crème caramel*, or fruit for dessert, then digestifs, probably cognac and liqueurs, then onto a café terrace for coffee and more brandy.

By now, the ice had begun to break, and jokes to fly. By the time coffee had been reached, everyone was having 'a reely great time'. Even Trudy had been heard to giggle, and once to say 'Wow!' When the bill arrived, Ida wanted to pay it, but this was dismissed as unthinkable by Henri. They wrestled over it for a while, which was helpful in breaking down the communication and cultural barriers between them.

As we left the restaurant, Ida whispered to me, 'He's a great guy, Monsieur Henri. When we first got to his fourth-rate, clapped out, shit-ridden hotel, I thought he was a stuck up French fag.'

'He's got a good sense of humour.'

'Sure thing. I've not laughed so much since my hubby Henry lost his denture on the dance floor.'

As we set off for Le Fiacre, they linked arms. The taxi was

crowded, so Henri got Ida on his knee, which brought them even closer, physically and emotionally. Even the cab-driver was, incredibly, in a happy mood, and recounted an ancient joke about an American who had asked for *Le tour* instead of *La tour*, and who'd been taken once around the square and deposited at his starting point. That rendered us hysterical.

At Le Fiacre (*Ici, on s'amuse; on joue; on rit; on boit!*), a noisy party was already in full blast.

Soon it was announced: 'Ladies and gentlemen, please pay careful attention! During each evening, the owner of this establishment will present gratuitously a magnum of champagne to the party which is manifesting itself to be the most joyous!'

We needed no encouragement. The atmosphere was already thick with garlic, body odours and alcohol. So dense you hardly needed to drink the stuff. But we piled in, happily ordered champagne for everyone, and prepared to dance and drink the night away – whilst manifesting the requisite gaiety. The chorus line of semi-nude dancing girls provoked giggles from the ladies, and detailed physiological appraisal from J-P. His diagnosis, but perhaps I misunderstood it, was that they were all fatally diseased. Fortunately, his medical vocabulary was incomprehensible. The girls certainly had considerable difficulty with their high kicks, and most had failed to shave their armpits. Still, the audience was tolerant and they succeeded in being titillating. Then audience participation. We sang:

> *Boire un petit coup, c'est agréable*
> *Boire un petit coup, c'est doux.*
> *Mais il ne faut pas rouler dessous la table...*

suiting the action to the words. We played games requiring couples to change hats in time to accordion music, and, best of all, games which involved everyone kissing everyone else. From time to time, quarrels broke out and insults were exchanged. We were expected to behave like naughty, overtired children at a birthday party. Provided you'd had enough to drink, it was great fun. Everyone danced with everyone else, and you changed partners every few minutes. We shouted greetings to strangers. Sweat poured off us all. The Gauloises smoke made us blink and wipe our eyes, but that may have been from laughing so much. Time passed … we ordered another bottle … more time passed. We sang:

Chevaliers de la table ronde
Goûtons voir si le vin est bon
Goûtons voir, oui, oui, oui
Goûtons voir non, non, non,
Goûtons voir si le vin est bon…

We ordered another bottle in order to decide whether it was 'oui' or 'non'. Then we danced again. Ida and Henri could be seen together doing the java, a sexy ritual inherited from the *bals musettes* at the turn of the century. (As you arrived, you shouted 'ça va?', to your friends, which became 'cha va?' the name of the dance.) They were undoubtedly carrying on lively conversation, but in what language and with how much mutual comprehension was unclear. One exchange was:
'Listen, why don't you take your jacket off?'
'*Comment?*'
'Take off your coat.'
'Soon I take off trousers!'
'Fine by me.'
Soon, we were ready to order another bottle, because singing and dancing are thirsty work. Then we sang:

Savez vous planter les choux,
A la mode de chez nous?

And we answered our question
'We'll plant cabbages with our feet!' and, '*On les plante avec*

157

la tête…' knocking our heads on the floor to suit the action to the words. The next verse was: 'We'll plant them with our pricks!' which only gentlemen were able to mime. We then ordered another bottle – the last – before wishing everyone *adieu*, and *bonne nuit*, and kissing everyone yet again, more slowly this time, implying that kissing was not an '*adieu*' but rather a 'hello'. Wiping laughter, tears and sweat from our eyes, we limped out into fresh air.

This time, at two in the morning, our taxi driver was surly. He was insistent that no more than four passengers could legally go with him, and thus, as it happened, Ida and Henri were left to take a separate cab, telling us, as we sped away that we were to order a dozen oysters each for their breakfasts, preferably no. 3s.

'Don't be long, Mom!' shouted Trudy anxious at being left with two men.

'See you guys soon,' Ida replied.

At Au Pied de Cochon, the famous restaurant, there were problems in securing a table for five, and an argument developed. Mutual love and good fellowship began to fade and dissolve. Without much enthusiasm we ordered breakfast, watching for the arrival of the two missing members of our party. As we struggled through greasy onion soup with grated cheese piled on to it, J-P began to talk to me in French about his problems with Ann-Sophie who, contrary to an earlier version, was, alas, strongly opposed to their sleeping together.

'I have explained to her that if she regards it as a mortal sin, all she need do is confess on Sunday, and her place in Heaven will not be placed in jeopardy.'

'So she is a virgin?'

'Of course. I would not wish to sleep with her if she were not.'

It was far too late – or too early – to question the elusive logic of this doctrine. By now, it had become apparent that Ida and Henri were not joining us on the final lap of our marathon *nuit de plaisir* – and who could blame them? They had presumably found better things to do.

Restless and bored by this French conversation, Trudy began to flirt with a group of American sailors on an adjacent table.

'Waddayouseguys doing in a sad dump like this?' she asked.

'Waiting for you, honey. Where d'you come from?'

'New York.'

'So do we. Come over here, and sit with us. We've got lots to talk about.'

'Haven't you got any girls of your own?'

'Why would we want them, when we can have you?'

'What all of you?'

'Just one at a time, honey, one at a time.'

Introduction of a competitive element provoked J-P into retaliation. In a single combined reflex action he took Trudy's hand, gave her his devastating smile, drew her close, and put his other hand up her skirt. Who could have resisted this combined assault?

During the taxi ride home to the Victoire, I slept. Confused dreams of my lovely Jacqueline, with the open smile, were interrupted by revolting noises from J-P and Trudy locked together on the back seat. Falling into bed, my last conscious thought was of having found myself yet again without a girl, that the skills required for the French art of seduction, which I had been practising so assiduously, still eluded me.

After what seemed only a few seconds, Henri shook me awake. It was five in the morning. 'William, I have come in the night to ask for your help.'

'What? What do you want?'

For a moment I couldn't even think who he was.

'I have at last fallen in love. For nearly forty years, I have been waiting hopefully for this to happen, and enfin, it has come to me.'

'Congratulations and good-night.'

'No wait, William. She is wonderful. We have been making

love for hours. In countless different positions. I have never experienced desire like it before. I have taken many potions to try to produce more excitement and fulfilment but now I have had all that. No, I mean that we have had all that, because she too has been experiencing sublime ecstasy.'

'How do you know?'

'She has told me. She has described the beauty and wonder of it all.'

'How did you understand her English?'

'With her, I understand everything.'

'Why have you woken me up?'

In my semi-conscious state, falling asleep again every few seconds, I was having great difficulty in speaking French. Henri shook me again.

'Listen, William, you must help me. I am asking you seriously as a friend. I have decided I can't be separated from her, now that I have found her. They have to leave tomorrow, for their tickets have been booked. So I am going with them.'

'Where are you going?'

'William, stay awake for a few minutes. I am going with them to New York. She has a home there, and I will live with them. Later I will come back and sell the hotel.'

'What about her own Henry? The one she has in New York?'

My enquiry was an absurdly feeble one, but the whole dialogue was crazy anyway.

'She says not to worry about him. They each live their own lives. I shall be Henri II. He was a great King of France, you know. He married Catherine de Medici, but he loved Diane de Poitier...'

'Never mind the history lesson. What about Maman?'

'I know I shall soon begin to feel guilty. But I have consecrated my whole life to looking after her. Now, aged nearly forty, I have to begin to live my own life. A great opportunity has come to me and, if I reject it, I may never get another chance.'

'What about your hotel?'

160

'I have fallen out of love with my hotel. Nor does she love me any more. It has been a long and passionate relationship, but now the time has come for us to part.'

'But, Henri, what will happen, practically speaking?'

'Maman will run it well. She always has, really. I just stand there and talk to people. I don't really accept any responsibility. For me, the hotel's just a waste of time. There's nothing in it for me. *Autant pisser dans un violon* – I might as well piss in a violin. William, please stay awake.'

'What do you want me to tell her?'

'You must give her this letter. I can't face her myself. Give it to her at noon. The nightwatchman will stay until then to operate the reception. He's very reliable. By then, we'll have gone, and I will be free and living a new life.'

'What about money?'

'I've taken some from the bag. And I have explained it to her in the letter. It is my money anyway. I'm going now and you can go back to sleep. Thank you for introducing me to Madame Ida. Thank you for helping me find true love. Thank you for your friendship. You know,' he said reflectively, his excitement suddenly evaporating, 'I've never had a high opinion of the Anglo-Saxon race, but now I find I've got a good English friend, and a wonderful American lover. Au revoir, William. We'll meet again, soon.'

Before I knew what to think about all this, whether to tell him he'd hate America, whether to laugh or cry, I had fallen unconscious again.

On waking, with sun bursting into my bedroom, our *nuit de gaîeté* seemed like a bad dream. Henri's visit had surely been part of that nightmare created by gastric punishment and physical exhaustion. No, that was disproven by his envelope on my bedside table, addressed 'Maman' in his precise handwriting. What a stupid way of spending an evening! Now there was a worse day to follow. Henri's adventure might have seemed miraculous to him, but the responsibility he'd thrust on me was unsustainable. Maman would throw a gigantic wobbly. She'd go into a screaming rage. Particularly as her money had been taken. She'd blame me, and would throw me into the street, bag and baggage. The gendarmerie would be summoned to carry me off to prison. Alternatively, she might collapse, leaving me to run her bloody hotel.

I washed and shaved slowly and carefully to postpone my fearful moment of descent into crisis, emotion and shouting, a scene so relished in France. A sense of nausea began to overcome me, and the flavour of onion soup returned as an ill omen. As my watch showed midday there was no excuse for further delay. I opened my bedroom door and listened. The hotel seemed quiet, although stairs creaked as usual.

At reception in his impressive marble pillared hall, Monsieur Henri stood, as usual, behind his desk. He was unshaven, and there were dark rings under his eyes. He had omitted to knot his silver tie. He watched me silent and unsmiling as I stumbled down his staircase. As I drew near, he leaned over and took his envelope from my hand.

'You won't be needing this, William.'

'You didn't go?'

'As you see.'

'Why not?'

'To leave the Victoire became hopelessly impossible. I had determined to do it, but I lost all my courage at the last moment.'

'I'm very sorry, Henri.'

'It is clear that I shall never see her again: the only creature in the whole world I have ever truly loved.'

'You still have your hotel.'

'For me, it represents no longer a historic victory, but a personal defeat.'

'I'm sorry, Henri.'

'You are a good friend, William.'

Silently, we shook hands, and he said:

'Now that we have become friends, I think we should call each other "*tu*" not "*vous*".'

162

I stood there reflecting on the impossibility of Henri's finding and keeping a true, faithful, corporeal lover. Whoever he found, his lifetime, bitter-sweet, demanding relationship with the Victoire would come between them as might a jealous mistress, a creature once young and beautiful, now a harridan, shrieking out to him about his responsibilities to her – responsibilities he could not or would not ever escape.

Today was to be my last in Paris. All the golden months – July, August and September - had slipped away and suddenly, it was *fin de saison*. Leaves on the chestnut trees along the Seine were turning to flame, and days dwindling down to a precious few. Pavement cafés were emptying, tables and chairs would soon be cleared away. Galéries Lafayette had abandoned tourist souvenirs, and switched to students' pencil-boxes – and satchels called, unaccountably, *'serviettes'*. Notices everywhere signalled *'rentrée des classes'*. Ice-cream vendors were preparing to roast chestnuts, and porno post-card salesmen had disappeared to count their takings. All the birds of passage were getting ready to fly away, and so, reluctantly, was I.

As a parting gesture J-P had invited me to lunch in his medical school refectory. When we were standing in the queue to collect our trays, he said, 'If you could remain in Paris until next month, William, you would have been an honoured guest at my wedding.'

'You're joking!'

'Not at all.'

'Who is your fiancée?'

'It is, of course, Ann-Sophie, who, as you know, is very beautiful.'

'Congratulations! I hope you'll both be very happy.'

'That is totally assured.'

'Shall you take an apartment?'

'Ultimately. But it depends on the dowry in our marriage contract, which has not yet been finally negotiated. For the present, we shall live in her parents' house, which is a grand establishment.'

163

'Yes, I remember.'

'Ah, you know it?'

'You took me there once for dinner.'

'Did I? Well, I don't remember. When you return to Paris you must come and visit us.'

'That will not be until next summer at the earliest.'

'Really? By then, our son will be aged six months.'

'Renewed congratulations!'

'Ann-Sophie is a young and healthy girl with wide hips, so I do not anticipate any delivery problems.'

'What has been the reaction of Ann-Sophie's parents?'

'They were not inclined to be "*sympa*" at first, but now they've become used to the idea they are absolutely delighted.'

'Have you completed all your examinations?'

'No, but between ourselves, William, I don't anticipate many problems in future. You see "*le paternel*" – Ann-Sophie's father – has become Chairman of the Board of Examiners at my medical school.'

'I see.'

What I did see was that whilst Monsieur Henri, so worldly, and sophisticated in his way, was finding the problems of girls, love and marriage insurmountable, J-P was demonstrating the capacity to organise all those aspects of life along simple traditional lines. A lovely wife with money, a home, a child, his medical qualification, and soon no doubt, a job and a future career were being put in place with easy precision. That was the way to prosper in the world. Which example, I wondered, would I follow?

When we reached the cash desk, I said, 'You must let me pay my share.'

'Pay for it all, would you, William? I haven't got any money with me.'

Lunch at the refectory was *blanquette de veau* washed down with a coarse and fruity *rouge*. Unlimited quantities. Students brought tin boxes which they filled surreptitiously, to be reheated for supper. Afterwards, replete with food, wine and friendship,

J-P and his friends talked about life and love, with special reference to Ann-Sophie's interesting condition. Then we pondered the influence of the Seine on Paris.

'It is a central artery along which life flows.'

'It is a mirror of life; when you look into it, you see yourself reflected.'

'But you do not see yourself as a static being. You see your life streaming down towards open sea.'

'The banks of the Seine are traditionally a preserve of young lovers. So that they can have privacy as they walk hand in hand, or embrace under the shadows of bridges...'

After this tremendous interlude, violent handshaking, and chorused shouts of '*Adieu! Adieu!*', I set off on a lingering stroll from the Medical School back to Hôtel Victoire, far across the river on the Right Bank. My route would take me along Quai des Grands Augustins, across Pont Neuf to Tuileries then Rue de Rivoli, Place de l'Opéra, Boulevard Haussmann, and finally ... Hôtel Victoire. During my journey, I would fix in mind these final views of *la ville lumière* – autumnal, elegant and splendid – to take away with me.

For my days dwindle down to the precious few,
September, November...
And these few precious days, I'll spend with you...

For me the days had suddenly dwindled down, not to a few, but to half of one. A terrible sense of lost opportunity oppressed me. Boulevard St Germain brought back a fading memory of quatorze juillet, Jacqueline, wine and roses, kisses...

Directly in front of Ecole de Medicine was the bench on which we'd been sitting back to back when she'd rushed off. Preoccupied with my lost love, I crashed into a café chair and banged my leg. Struggling to get up, I thought I saw her walking alone on the opposite pavement. I'd often imagined seeing her, but this time it was for real.

'Jacqueline, d'you remember me? We met on the *quatorze*...'
'But of course, William, I remember. Listen,' she said in English:

Though the night was made for loving
And the day returns too soon,
We'll go no more a roving,
By the light of the moon...

'You've been learning English.'
'Certainly. And I've been hoping to meet you to show it off.'
'And I've been hoping to meet you. Why did you disappear like that?'
'I was afraid...'
'What?'
'...that you were a bold seducer.'
'I'm not at all bold, but let's sit down and have a drink.'
'Not now, William, I can't. But let's meet tomorrow.'
'Tomorrow I shall be back in England.'
'My poor William. That is terrible for you.'
Sadly, we kissed and parted.
On that last night, dinner chez Robert was a lonely affair, and my gorgeous waitress, Sylvie, provided poor consolation. When she bent to serve the *specialité de la maison* her low cut black satin dress fell open, hinting delicately at delights one had missed.
'I'm sorry you're leaving, Monsieur William, but I have been enchanted to make your acquaintance.'
'Me too, Sylvie. You've looked after me very well.'
'I'd have done more for you Monsieur William, if you'd asked me.'
After multiple handshaking with the family, the last act was a quick cuddle with Sylvie in the street. Yes, my recollection was correct, her black sateen bum was beautifully shaped, round and firm. Why hadn't I spent the whole summer caressing it?
There was time for a quick nightcap at Bar Victoire. Ann-Marie, Henri's special friend, gave me a wink and came over to

166

cadge a drink in exchange for a few flirtatious jokes. Tonight, she was unusually talkative.

'Maybe I could come back with you to America, Monsieur William, if you'd package me in your kitbag.'

'I'm not a G.I., Ann-Marie. I'm British.'

'Really? Well, maybe I could come there in your suitcase. The British like fucking, don't they?'

'They certainly do.'

'So would I do well in London?' She showed me a length of black-stockinged thigh. 'They say prices are good.'

'You wouldn't like London – there's no *vin blanc* there.'

'Really? Then I won't come. I'll stay here and marry Monsieur Henri instead.'

'I'll tell him you have proposed to him.'

'That is very kind of you, Monsieur William, and I shall try and find some way of rewarding you.'

In the morning, Monsieur Henri stepped out in front of his reception desk, for a special leave-taking. He was wearing his friendly but professional smile.

'Are you glad the season is nearly over?' I asked him politely.

'Yes, for it has been a summer of some disappointments, I admit. When autumn, comes, I decide to sell my hotel and go to the country. But when the spring comes, I realise that the Victoire is my only true love, and that I shall never find another.'

So he was reconciled to his fate. This confirmed that his hotel and his terrible mother would come between him and any other 'true love', and he would have to be content with those weekly sexual emissions at no. 122, which he claimed, kept him healthy.

'At least, the Victoire will always be faithful to you.'

Was there a small tear glistening in Henri's eye?

'Do you think that my American lover will ever come back to Paris?'

'Of course.'

As if physically to impede any such event, Maman waddled into the hall, her face distorted. It was a smile of farewell. She pulled me towards her for *la bise*: left cheek, right cheek, left cheek again... How long must this go on? Finally she released me with a firm push towards the double doors. There, Henri and I stood together.

'*Au revoir*, William.'

'*Au revoir*, Henri and thank you for your warm welcome to Paris.'

'William, you've forgotten. You and I use "*tu*" when we speak to one another.'

'Tu *as raison* ... *je* te *remercie pour* ton *acceuil chaleureux*.'

'You'll come back next year?'

'I hope so.'

'I'm sure you will. You'll come back and spend your whole life in France. You're almost a Frenchman now. Have a good journey.'

'Until next time, Henri.'

We shook hands once more. I shouldered my bag and set off for England.

On the morning after my absurd night in Montmartre, I woke late, after terrible nightmares. I'd been standing lost and alone in the centre of Place de la Bastille – or was it Place du Tertre? – and all my Paris friends and acquaintances had assembled around me in a ring. At first I couldn't understand what they were shouting; then I realised they were taunting me about my inability to speak their beautiful, eloquent language. Henri himself was there, his Maman, the Dubois family, J-P, Monsieur Robert, Ann-Sophie, la Baronne and Ann-Marie. They were laughing at the incapacities of the English, their lack of elegance, sensitivity and just about every other desirable human quality. They left me in no doubt that in their joint, considered view the English were an inadequate race, and I was a particularly inadequate specimen. The best thing I could do was to go back whence I had come and never, ever set foot in the Hexagon again.

My watch showed ten-thirty. I was suffering all the classical symptoms of stupid, sentimental self-indulgence: nausea, aching stomach, spinning head, foul mouth. So much for nights of gaiety and pleasure. I'd missed breakfast, and the morning refuse collectors had come and gone without disturbing me. Or perhaps they'd stayed in bed – and who could blame them, for rain streamed down the windows and Paris looked miserable. But it was appropriate weather for a funeral. Ten-thirty already! And Henri's funeral was at eleven. I staggered out of bed and into the bathroom. This was my last chance of confronting J-P.

By the time I'd packed my bag, changed to a mid-afternoon flight, and checked out of The Georges V, it was eleven. In the Avenue, taxis were elusive, but I finally made it, by running wildly across traffic and jumping into one. Rain and sweat streamed from me.

Breathlessly, I shouted, '*Basilique Nôtre Dame des Victoires, s'il vous plait.*'

As the driver gave no sign of having heard, I repeated myself and got a grudging, '*D'accord!*'

Traffic moved slowly in the rain and it was nearly noon by the time we got there. The church wasn't near Hôtel Victoire, but in a different *quartier*. But by chance (or *not* by chance), Henri's funeral, it seemed, was to be staged in another building celebrating another victory. When we got there I was writhing with impatience but, with an effort, paid off the taxi and ran into the nave. An organ was playing softly. There wasn't any coffin or funeral service in progress. The big church was almost empty. Where was everyone? Running desperately outside again, I just caught sight of Ann-Marie and the doctor together under an umbrella, heading across the street. Ann-Marie appeared tiny, dwarf-like against the doctor, whose professional dignity would have been apparent a mile away. Summoning all my reserves I ran to intercept them.

'Excuse me...'

They both turned and stared back without sign of recognition.

'*Excusez moi de vous déranger...*

I began to babble.

'Do you remember me? My name is William Soames. I was a friend of Monsieur Henri's years ago. I came to see you yesterday at the hospital. You told me about his funeral today. I wanted to attend, but I got delayed. I'm sorry to have missed the service. Have I missed the service?'

They looked at me as they had done in my dream, and I again became conscious of the inadequacies of the Anglo-Saxon race.

'Yes, you've certainly missed it, whoever you are.'

'What about the burial, I mean the grave?'

'No burial. No grave. Henri is being transported to a crematorium in accordance with his own wishes. He was not a believer.'

Was all that true, I began to wonder, or was their hostility concealing something? Was I probing into some unimaginable conspiracy. For a few moments my time frame slipped and I believed that Henri was still alive, but had gone into hiding from his terrible Maman because she was still struggling to get him to marry the rich widow with two children. Because I was refusing to go away we just stood staring at one another.

Then, ungraciously, the doctor said, 'Do you want to come into this café for a few moments? Madame Rouget is tired after the strain and needs to take some refreshment.'

The doctor commanded two coffees, leaving me to add my own order. We sat in uncomfortable silence until the drinks came. After I'd taken a gulp to fortify myself, I tried again.

'Doctor Pontin, do you remember that we met about thirty years ago, when I was staying at the Hôtel Victoire? You came there often to see Henri. We met many times. You were very welcoming, and introduced me to many friends in Paris.'

'I regret, Monsieur, that I do not remember you.'

'We went once to Place du Tertre, with other people, and you told me about your ambition to become a doctor.'

'I have been there many times, but I do not remember the occasion to which you refer.'

'You took me to dine with friends. There was an accident en route. You told me I was in need of a sentimental education, and you provided me with an opportunity to fall in love with one of three beautiful daughters. You yourself were about to marry one of them. You had announced your engagement. She was the eldest and most beautiful. Her name was...'

Infuriatingly it eluded me. The doctor unsmilingly shook his head.

'You are totally mistaken, Monsieur. What is evident is that you are confusing me with someone else. Henri had many friends. He was always a very sociable person.'

During this exchange Ann-Marie had been showing clear signs of impatience.

'None of this is at all interesting for me – on this day, particularly.'

She looked at her watch.

In desperation, I said, 'And I remember that your Christian name is Jean-Philippe.'

'Certainly not! It is Jean-Pierre. I am telling you finally, monsieur, you are making a confusion of identity. You seem to know nothing about me although you pretend to do so. It is true I was married to a beautiful spouse, but she died many years ago, and I am a widower. Such is your confusion that I must invite you to consider again whether you ever knew the late Henri Rouget. You are a foreigner: an American apparently. Is it not possible that you are a little lost in Paris? We are surprised you should impose yourself upon us at this time, a sad one for Madame...'

'I'm sorry but...'

'Perhaps it is the death of someone else which has disturbed you.'

'I'm very sorry, perhaps it is.'

'So you have recently lost someone close to you?'

'Yes.'

'As a doctor of some experience, may I now counsel you to return home and rest quietly for, say, twenty-four hours. Perhaps you should take a sedative. You have the appearance of a person who has been enduring some psychological stress.' Neither Henri nor J-P, I decided, would ever condescend to recognise me. That left Ann-Marie, who looked at me with open hostility. Should I tell her I remembered how Henri had gone to see her at no. 122 to enjoy release of his psychological tensions? That I'd once rushed into the bedroom to find her and Henri in bed and apparently unconscious? That I'd seized her by the wrist to ascertain if she'd still had a pulse? I looked at her wrist as she held her coffee cup, and remembered the texture of it under my fingers.

'They are dead,' someone had shouted, 'but are they not beautiful?'

'They have committed suicide together. He was always a romantic!'

'What a scandal for the house!'

No, these were slices of history which could never be recalled.

Nor could I tell her that I'd been present at the Victoire during one terrible scene when Henri had confronted his Maman, telling her he couldn't marry anyone at the moment because Ann-Marie needed him to care for her. This had produced exclamations of horror and disgust, and a burst of vituperative vocabulary which had sent me scurrying to my Dictionary of Colloquial French. She had concluded: 'You will order that corrupt little English pig' (that was me) 'back to his filthy country and you will do as I say, Henri, and that's the end of the matter.' But now it had emerged that he hadn't done as she said; that somehow, in the end, he'd summoned the strength to escape from her power and live happily – it appeared – with his Ann-Marie until death did them part.

Nor could I remind Ann-Marie that she'd once invited herself to come away with me if I could package her in my kit-bag. Nor that Henri had told me her life history – her terrible shaming as a 'collaborator' during the Occupation.

No, none of these episodes could be cited as evidence of our previous acquaintance. They'd all become irredeemable events in my youthful Paris life. It now seemed a different life, a different world, peopled with different people. I couldn't recapture the past via those I'd once known. Those who'd lived then had ceased to exist, and so, correspondingly, had I.

'Thank you, I will take your advice.'

With chilling formality, we all shook hands.

'*Au revoir Madame, au revoir Monsieur.*'

They both responded:

'*Adieu!*'

Next door to the café was a print shop called 'Yesterday and Today'. To escape from the driving rain I walked in and looked around. A woman seated at a desk stood up and asked whether she could help.

I said without thinking, 'I'm looking for something to take back home. A souvenir of my visit.'

'When you're back in America?'

'Is it that obvious?'

'Not really.'

When she smiled, I became aware she was attractive, tall with a pure line like a Modigliani model. I looked at conventional 'tourist' prints and my eye was caught by the famous Doisneau poster: *Le Baiser de l'Hôtel de Ville 1950*. Café tables on a terrace. A couple caught in an instant of spontaneous and intense emotion. His arm was around her shoulder. Her head tilted back for the kiss. Carefree, unthinking love! I'd read somewhere that the picture had been posed for the camera, but who cared? That had been my Paris era – when men wore jaunty berets, girls silk stockings. In the background was the city hall, but it might have represented Hôtel Victoire.

'I'll take one of those. Paris as it was. Not yesterday, but the day before. It was a time when life was sweet, but you couldn't know.'

She laughed readily.

'No, not quite. What made it so sweet for you?'

'It was romantic, like Doisneau.'

'I don't think Paris has changed so much. What is much more

likely, Monsieur, if you will permit me to say so, is that it's you that's changed, over the years since 1950. "Evolved" – as we say, in French. You should come back, spend more time here, and get to know it as it is now.'

'Yes, I must do that.'

She carefully rolled the poster and fitted it into a cardboard tube. I paid her and we shook hands. Not everyone in Paris, it seemed, was hostile. It was comforting to experience some personal warmth at however trivial a level. Although I hadn't eaten all day, I began to feel better.

The cab journey to Roissy was slow but, looking at my watch, I reckoned I should still arrive early for my flight. That allowed me to slip into another daydream which located Henri, J-P and Ann-Marie in Doisneau's Paris. This confusion of fiction and reality was, I knew, a false one, but I didn't care. Then the image of that loving kiss made me suddenly realise that I had ceased to think obsessively about the most important character in my historical Parisian romance: Jacqueline, the true heroine in my personal story – the girl with an open smile and the sweet tasting kisses which I'd come to know so well. For the last month I'd thought about her every day – no, every hour – wallowing in my loneliness.

Once upon a time, as storytellers begin, many years ago, I'd sent cards from New York to all my Paris friends whose addresses I could find. Henri's reply had been about Ida. Sometime afterwards, I'd got one back in unfamiliar handwriting from 'Jacqueline'. At first, I hadn't been able to put a face to that name. Then I remembered the tall, elegant girl I'd met and kissed on *quatorze juillet.* Her letter had taken conventional form, expressing regret we'd never had a chance to meet again in Paris, but that she was coming to New York because she'd got an important job as an interpreter for the United Nations. Maybe I would have time to show her 'my' city? I would find, she'd added, that her command of English had progressed and we would be able to continue our agreeable conversation about the great Lord Byron and all the other important English poets whose work she so much admired.

Now I remembered how I'd arranged to meet her at La Guardia airport and show her New York, which at that time was still new to me. In retrospect, life had seemed easy then. Full of affection, laughter and companionship. I remembered our first apartment and our passionate love-making – in both languages – and our marriage and how our happy life together had begun, and continued until – how long was it now? – a month?

Every year on 14th July we'd talk about how we first met and kissed in Place de la Bastille.

'Soon, William,' she would say, 'we will go back to Paris together, to dance in the square, and pretend that we are meeting for the first time. And you will recite Byron to me, and we will travel about Paris on the autobus.'

'Let's go there for the 14th July next year.'

But we never did. Instead of going back, we'd always gone forward. We'd danced our way hand in hand through time and place from *quatorze juillet* in Place Bastille to last month in Washington Square. But now Jacky and I would go no more a-roving together so late into the night by the light of the moon. According to the Byronic muse, which she'd so much admired, love must find rest, and she'd found rest after her short but terrible final illness. For me, Byron had lost his appeal. I'd not yet found rest, and so Jacky had not yet become part of my Paris memory-bank, but remained a living, constant companion by my side.

And yet ... I had to recognise that all my happy memories of her were now beginning to fade and there was no known route along which I could recapture those memories in the way I'd sought to live again my memories of Henri and Henri's world in Paris. And anyway, that attempt had failed. That's the way with memories, I'd learned. Trying to recapture them is doomed to failure. It's better not to try.

My cab had reached Roissy, so I got out, paid the driver and went to the check-in.